HIRE A CUDDLER

HOW TO WIN AT LOVE

HOPE FORD

HAVEN

I HIRED A PROFESSIONAL CUDDLER.

I shake my head from side to side as I stand here, staring up at the ten-story hotel and trying not to run.

I hate this. Heck, I hate everything about it, but I know I have to do something because I can't keep going the way I am.

I'm twenty-five years old. I've never hugged another person, never said I love you, and every attempt at dating ends when a man reaches for my hand or tries to get close to me.

My therapist calls it intimacy avoidance, and after years of therapy, this seems like a last attempt at healing. I can even sense the desperation from my therapist when she suggested I try this.

I pull my shoulders back, stop fidgeting, and pretend I'm on a job instead of walking into an uncomfortable situation. I'm a plus-size model, and I can usually fake the confidence for photoshoots, walking runways, and modeling gigs. My plan is to treat this the same way.

I walk into the fancy hotel, stop in my tracks as it hits me, and wonder what the hell am I doing? This is a hotel, and I'm about to go into a room with a perfect stranger. Tense, I put my hand to my forehead and think about how this is not very smart of me because people are going to think I'm some kind of hooker or something.

However, this is definitely not the type of place that rents the room by the hour because it is one of Jasper's elite hotels.

I'm about to walk out when a man approaches me. "Haven Weston?"

My forehead creases as I stare at the man. He seems harmless enough. He's shorter than me and smaller in stature. Definitely not a threat. But does he recognize me from modeling or from the profile intake sheet I had to fill out for a cuddler?

I point to myself. "I'm Haven. Are you Victor?"

He nods his head but doesn't reach his hand out. Maybe he knows that I wouldn't want to take it, but he remains standing with his hands in his pockets, just smiling at me.

"Yeah, I'm Victor, and I thought I'd meet you out here for the first appointment. It usually freaks people out a little to be meeting at a hotel. So the first floor of the hotel has restaurants, boutique shops, and a few other businesses, and we have our offices here too. Will you follow me?"

I nod, my fake confidence already starting to wear. I follow him down the hallway and stop outside an office. He doesn't attempt to open it; he just gestures to the door. "So through here are our offices. I like to sort of explain things before going in because I've found that a lot of people that visit us don't like surprises. The first room is just a room. There is a couch, two chairs and a desk in the corner. The next room over is a room with a television, couch, and more chairs. We have another room that has a bedroom that is used for cuddling."

Before I can interrupt, he continues. "Everything is on the up and up here. We move slowly. Today, we'll just get to know each other. Slowly, we'll work through things until you're comfortable. It can be simple hand-holding, massage, meditation, talking through what you're feeling, and eventually cuddling. But we move at your pace."

I have a thousand questions rolling through my head, but I can't form a sentence to save my life, so I just clear my throat and nod my head.

He opens the door, walks in, and holds it open for me. I don't know what I was expecting. Maybe some gaudy bedroom with silk sheets and the stench of sweat or something. That's exactly what I was expecting. I have built this up so much in my head that I've twisted it to something it's not.

I'm here for legitimate therapy. It sounds insane to think that cuddling with someone is going to help me, but I have to give it a shot. Nothing else has done any good, so I need to go at this with an open mind.

Victor waves his hand around the room. "Sit wherever you'll feel most comfortable."

I avoid the couch and sit down in the chair that seats one person. Victor grabs a clipboard and sits in the chair across from me.

"Tell me about yourself, Haven."

I start by saying "uh" and then go into the spiel I always use at work. "I'm a professional plus size model. I'm twenty-five years old and from Whiskey Run. I love reading, volunteering, and walking."

He smiles at the paper in his hand as he takes notes. "Okay, now tell me about you… why are you here?"

My voice gets softer and less sure. "Because I have intimacy avoidance."

"Why?"

I scrunch my nose up. "Why?"

He nods, still looking down at the paper, but I'm just not comfortable talking about this. Instead of answering him, I ask my own questions. "How long have you been doing this, Victor?"

"A year."

I nod and lean forward with my arms crossed over my chest. "And is the success rate with your patients high?"

"It is for the people that put in the work," he says, looking at me down his nose. He obviously doesn't like being questioned, but I don't care. I can't imagine ever being comfortable enough with him to actually let him touch me or cuddle with me.

"And what does that mean… put in the work?"

His smile is tight. "Well, for starters, answer questions."

I nod and blurt out in frustration, "I'm here because I had a shitty upbringing and I don't trust people. How's that?"

If anything, his smile deepens, and it makes me feel like I did something right in his eyes. "That's good. That's a start at least. Let's talk about schedules. I want to see you twice a week."

"Twice a week?" I repeat, surprised.

He nods. "Yeah, I think it's a good idea."

I shrug, already dreading the next appointment. "Okay."

He nods. "Okay, how about I give you a tour of the other offices and then we'll convene again next week?"

I nod and follow him, trying not to let the disappointment set in. I don't know what I was hoping for, maybe an instant connection where I felt a closeness with another person. Where I felt safe and maybe even was on the receiving end of a hug or something, but I don't feel anything but numb… and ridiculous.

2

———

KING

"WHO IS SHE?" I repeat to the woman behind the desk.

She looks at me wide-eyed, shaking her head. "Sir, like I said, I can't give out guest information."

I'm about to pull money out of my wallet when the woman lifts her chin at me and holds her hand up. "Forget it. You're wasting your time."

Even though I'm pissed off, I am a little impressed. Most people don't tell me no. Either because of my size or my name, I almost always get what I want.

I put my wallet back into my pocket, and with a nod, I walk away and take a seat in the lobby of the hotel. I lean forward, elbows on my knees, and glance down the hall in the direction where I last saw the woman.

I noticed her as she was walking into the hotel. I had just left a meeting next door, and I couldn't take my eyes off her. She's beautiful, and there was no way I was going to let her out of my sight. I've never had to chase a woman down before, but that's exactly what I did.

As soon as I got through the front door of the hotel, I saw her walking down the hall with a man that either doesn't realize how beautiful the woman is beside him or they just met. There was an awkwardness in their stance, and I'm hoping that they are not together. If they are, they won't be for long. I'm not a homewrecker, but if he doesn't have a ring on her finger, then she's fair game.

I keep watching down the hallway, trying to figure out where she went or who she could be. Is she here on vacation? Is she staying at the hotel for work? The first floor has businesses; does she work in one of the offices?

The longer I sit here, the more intense my need is to see her again.

I feel as if I'm barely hanging on. I'm about to go up to the front desk again when I see the woman walking slowly down the hall with the same man. I stand up, hands fisted at my sides, and openly stare at her. For a second, I'd wondered if I'd worked it up in my head and maybe she wasn't as beautiful as I thought. I had seen her from a distance before, but now, only a few feet away from her, it's very clear that she is more than beautiful. And she has a body made for sin.

I want to reach out and stop her, but I don't. I try to eavesdrop on their conversation, and it's obvious their relationship, if it even is one, is a new one. It's all very formal, and I let out a sigh of relief to figure out that she's not on a date with this man. I hear them talk about seeing each other again in two days, and when the man opens his arms, as if expecting a hug, I almost move toward them.

I can't stand here and let some man put his arms around her. I don't know how or why I feel so strongly about her already, but I do.

I'm already on the move but stop suddenly when instead of hugging the man, the woman puts her hand out to shake instead. I watch as they shake hands and then watch the woman disappear.

I'm riddled with indecision. Do I follow her? There's a vulnerability about her, and I don't know if she will be open to just being approached by some stranger on the street. The man she was with is hanging around and I watch as he approaches another woman. They shake hands, talk, and then start walking down the hall again. Before they go into a closed door, I call out, "Excuse me, sir. Can I talk to you for a minute?"

He nods, looking at me with his eyebrows raised. "Go on in, Candace. I'll be with you in just a minute."

As soon as the door closes behind her, I step up to the man. I'm easily a foot taller and have at least a hundred pounds on him. "What's your name?"

He leans his head back to look up at me, and his eyes are wide as he stutters, "Victor."

I nod. "Victor, I'm Ridge Beckett. You know me?"

He may not have recognized me by sight, but he sure as hell recognizes the name. "Yeah, I've heard of you."

I nod again. "Right, tell me about the woman. Who is she?"

He points to the closed door. "Candace—"

I cut him off. "Not her. The woman that was with you before. Who is she?"

He thinks about it. "You mean Haven Weston? Big girl, blond hair."

My nostrils flare at the way he says *big girl* like

it's a bad thing or something. "Haven Weston. Tell me about her and what she was doing here with you."

"Uhhh, well, I don't think I should give out that information…"

I cross my arms over my massive chest, and I don't have to say a word before he starts rambling. "Her name is Haven Weston. She's a fashion model, and today was our first appointment. She has intimacy issues, and I'm helping her with those."

I reach for him before I can stop myself. I grab him by the front of his shirt and pull him close to me. "What the fuck does that mean?"

He doesn't struggle. "I'm a professional cuddler. I help people. I, uh, uh, didn't touch her."

When he admits he didn't touch her, I release him, and he leans over, hands on his knees as he sucks in air. He acts as if he's been running a marathon or something. "You didn't touch her?" I ask, wanting to hear it again.

He raises up, pulling at the front of his shirt. "No, I didn't touch her. She is not comfortable with any intimacy… I barely got a handshake out of her. She's been going to therapy for years, and this is her last resort."

"Why? Who did this to her?" I ask and then shake my head. "Forget it, I'll find out on my own. When's her next appointment?"

He looks at me uneasily. "Thursday, but…"

"I'm going to be her next—what did you call it —cuddler?"

He holds his hands up, shaking his head. "What? No, I can't… you are not qualified…"

I cross my arms over my chest again and stare down at him. "You went to school for this? You have a degree for it?"

He chokes over the words. "There is a certification for it. It's a legitimate business."

He must not realize that I have business dealings every day—million dollar negotiations—and I pay attention to everything. "I noticed you said there is a certification for it, but you don't have one. Is that correct?"

He nods his head and purses his lips, and it's obvious he's lying.

"One phone call. That's all it will take. Are you certified?"

He clenches his eyes shut and shakes his head. "No. I failed the test, and I couldn't afford to take it again. I lied on the application."

"Okay, here's what we're going to do."

"What?"

"I'm going to pay to have you retake the test."

"It's a thousand dollars!" he exclaims.

I pull out my wallet and slowly count out two thousand dollars from my wallet and hold it out to him. He wants to take it, but he knows something is up. "What's the catch?"

"I'm taking over your appointments with Haven."

"But—"

I cut him off and continue. "And I won't tell anyone about your lack of a certificate as long as you pass your test and get qualified."

He reaches for the money and then stops, his conscience getting the best of him. "What's your deal with Haven?"

I'm not used to explaining myself, but I also want to make sure this works out. "I want to get to know her…"

"This is therapy… not a dating service. Can't you do this without—"

I cut him off. "You said she has intimacy issues, so no, I can't just approach her off the street. She'll be safe with me. I won't hurt her."

"Fuck." He grunts. "Fine." He takes the money, and even though he watched me count it, he counts it again. "Her next appointment is Thursday at one."

"You have until the end of the month to pass your test or I'm turning you in, Victor."

Without another word, I walk away from him, pulling my phone out of my pocket. I type in *Haven Weston*, determined to learn everything I can about her before Thursday.

3

———

HAVEN

I TOLD myself all week that I couldn't back out, and this is my last resort. I need to give it my all. I'm tired of having my guard up with everyone I meet. I've had my mind set with determination, but the day of my appointment, I start to talk myself out of it.

As I walk into the hotel, dread comes over me. I don't want to do this. I mean, yeah, of course, I'd love to cure my intimacy issues, but I can't see this helping me. The whole thing the other day with Victor was awkward, and it's not something I want to have to deal with again. I'm already convinced this is not going to work without even giving it a good try.

I know that canceling this late will probably

incur a cancellation fee, but I don't care. I'd rather pay the hundred dollars and just go home to deal with things on my own.

As I'm walking into the hotel, I see Victor pacing back and forth. As soon as he sees me, he stops. "Hello, Haven—"

Before he gets into it, I interrupt him. "I'm sorry, I should have called yesterday. I don't think this is going to work out, and I know you need to charge me a cancellation fee or whatever and that's fine, I completely understand."

"You can't quit… I mean, look, I'm actually out here because I had—I mean—have an emergency, and I had to call in another cuddler for your case. He's waiting for you now."

"But…" I start, and Victor is walking backward away from me. "So if you can go talk to him… if you need to cancel, just let him know."

"But…" I call after him, but he doesn't stop, and he's walking out the door without turning back.

I look down the hallway, and dread settles like a heavy ball in my stomach. Okay, so I guess I'll go in there and cancel my appointment. Easy peasy.

I slowly walk down the hallway, and when I get to the office door, I pull my shoulders back, take a deep breath, force a smile that I'm not feeling to my face, and knock.

The door opens instantly, and I take a step back as I lean my head back to look at the huge man standing in front of me.

He's tall with wide shoulders, and I take another step back. He looks to be in his late thirties or early forties, and he has muscles on top of muscles.

He's watching me closely. "Hello, Haven. My name is Ridge, but my family calls me King. Won't you come in?"

He takes a step back and gestures inside the room.

I know I should answer him or acknowledge him in some way, but I'm too busy looking at him. I've never seen a man as rugged yet handsome and put together as him. His jaw is strong and covered with a thin stubble. His hair is short on the sides, but the top hangs a little over his brow. His eyes, which are trained on me so hard that I feel like he can read my mind, are brown with gold speckles, making me want to stand on my tiptoes to get a closer look.

The thought freaks me out a little, and I take another step back so that I'm standing in the middle of the hallway. King still hasn't moved. It's like he's frozen in place, looking at me with patience.

"Haven," he says softly.

I wait for him to reach for me, and I know I'll freak out, but he surprises me when his hands fist at his sides and he continues to talk to me in a soothing voice. "I'm standing in for Victor today. If you're more comfortable out there, we can meet in the lobby if you prefer."

"Uh," I start, looking everywhere but at him.

My heart is racing, and my palms are getting sweaty. I try to say something, but I'm frozen in place, overwhelmed by everything I'm feeling right now. Why am I like this? Why am I reacting to him this way?

"Uh," I finally stutter. "Cancel. I need to cancel."

He shifts his weight from one foot to the other, and besides the way his shoulders tense a little, that's the only tell that he doesn't like what I'm saying. He leans against the open door. "Why would you cancel, Haven?"

I swear his tone drops an octave every time he says my name. "Because last time…"

I let my voice trail off, and King waits patiently

for me to continue. "Because I don't think this is going to help me, that's all."

He lifts his hand and runs it through his hair. "Yeah, but your appointment the other day was with Victor. Today your appointment is with me. Don't you think you should give me a chance?"

He pauses and looks at me with hope in his eyes. "I hope you'll give me a chance, Haven."

My hand goes to my stomach because it feels like butterflies are churning around in there. I don't know what this reaction is. I mean, yeah, the man is gorgeous, but he's my cuddler, someone hired to be here… it's not like a date or anything.

I'm quiet for so long, but King's voice is still calm and patient. "What about it, Haven? Give me an hour to change your mind?"

There's a part of me that wants to say no and run out of here, but something is stopping me. I stand fully erect, teetering on my high heels, and I know I need to make a decision. Hopefully, it's one I don't regret.

"Okay," I murmur.

He smiles, and it lights up his whole face. "Okay, you'll stay?"

I take a deep breath and let it out slowly. I try to

get my nerve up as I take one step toward him. I move slowly, and he does nothing to pressure me; he just stands there smiling. I take another step, and he nods his head encouragingly, and then I take another one. I'm right at the door, and he moves farther back, giving me a wide berth to enter the room.

I feel ridiculous. I don't usually react this way to people, not to this extent, but with him, it's like I can't seem to catch my breath.

He moves out of the way, using his foot to hold the door open. I walk past him, and I think I'm going to be okay until the door shuts behind me. I gasp at the slam, and then it's like an automatic reaction, and my thoughts start to spiral. The panic hits me in an instant, and I'm not sure what to do. I take a deep breath, trying to will away the way my heart starts to race, my body starts to tremble, and the shortness of breath takes over. In through my nose, out through my mouth. I repeat the mantra in my head, but it's no use.

I look at King in a panic. It's been years since I've had a panic attack, but here I am, having a breakdown in front of a man whose only offense is being too handsome.

He starts to reach for me, but he must see my

eyes widen because he stops and holds his hands up. He points to the chair. "Sit down, Haven."

I almost deny him until his voice comes at me with more sternness to it. "Sit down before you fall down."

I reach for the chair and sit down.

He sits across from me and leans forward. He's nowhere near touching me, but I swear I can feel the heat from his body even from here. "Look at me," he demands.

I am concentrating on breathing, and I lift my eyes to his as I take a deep breath. "Good girl," he says, and my body reacts in the strangest way.

My nipples pebble, and he nods his head. "Keep breathing and keep looking at me, sweetie."

I do as he says, mimicking the way he takes a deep breath in and lets it out slowly. I continue breathing as he talks to me. "You're doing so well, Haven. I'm so proud of you. Keep breathing, sweetie. In, out, in, out."

My breathing slows, and I start to pull myself together. I feel clammy and shaky, but I can tell that I am starting to calm.

"Keep it up. I'm going to get you something cool to drink."

He pulls out his phone and types into it. I wait

for him to get up, but he doesn't. He pockets his phone and continues to look at me with concern.

"I'm okay," I assure him.

He nods. "I know you are."

I put my hand to my head and hide behind it. "I'm so embarrassed. I haven't had a panic attack in a long time."

I have my eyes clenched closed, and I'm shaking my head. Never have I wished for the floor to open up and swallow me whole more than I do right now.

4

KING

FUCK, she's beautiful. I mean, I knew she was, but this close, where I can just reach out and touch her, she's an enigma. I've stared at her since I opened the door, and I should stop. I'm supposed to be a professional cuddler, and instead I'm looking at her like I want to make her mine. I try to look away, but I can't force myself to. "Don't be embarrassed."

She shrugs. "Gah, how could I not? I'm so sorry." She puts her hand on the arm of her chair. "I should go."

"No. Stay. Talk to me."

She doesn't move because there's a knock at the door.

"Come in," I call out.

I stand up as my driver walks into the room. He

has a drink carrier with four different drinks in one hand, and he's holding a bag in the other.

I block his view of Haven and take everything from him. "Thank you, Callan. That will be all."

He gives me a little smirk and then turns to walk out the door. I set the items on the table. "You want water, juice, soda, or a shot of whiskey?"

For the first time, a smile plays on her lips. "You had him bring whiskey?"

I return her smile. "Yeah, it calms the nerves."

"Yeah, but I need to drive home. I'll take the water, please."

I pull the water out of the cup holder, put a straw in it, and hand it to her. Very briefly, our hands touch, and my whole body reacts to it. I keep my eyes focused on her, and there's no hiding the fact that she felt it too.

I turn away to hide my smile and pull the rest of the items out of the bag and then hold the candy out to her. "Here you go."

Her mouth drops open. "You got me orange slices?"

Fuck, if she's going to react like this, I'd buy her the candied slices every day just to see her face light up like it is right now. "Yeah, do you like them?" I ask her, when in fact, I know they're her favorite. I did my research on her since I saw her the other day, and after stalking her social media, it was easy to figure out some of her favorites.

She takes the bag from me. "I love these." As she rips open the bag, she continues talking. "When I was growing up, my mom always had these around the house. She didn't buy food or anything else we needed, but she always made sure to have these."

I try to keep my face free of judgment even though what she said makes me want to take her in my arms and hold her until she forgets all about her past. It doesn't help that it is one that I can relate to in a way. I was a foster kid, and I know what neglect feels like, but I try not to think about it. I like to think I put it all behind me. All the neglect, abuse, sad times, all of it. That's why I worked so hard to make something of myself. I had to prove I was worthy.

She puts a candy in her mouth and chews it as she watches me. It almost feels like she can hear my thoughts by the way she tilts her head and looks at me.

I sit back down in the chair and rest my elbows on my knees. "Can you tell me what happened?"

She keeps chewing, and I continue. "Did I do

something to cause it?" I know I should feel guilty for doing this. I have no business posing as a cuddler. I researched it and got the basics, but in no way am I prepared for this. But even knowing that, I had to do it. I knew I couldn't get close to her any other way. All I can do is hope she forgives me when the time comes.

She tries to reassure me. "It wasn't anything you did."

"I don't believe you. It started when I closed the door. Do you have trouble with closed spaces?"

She shakes her head and grabs another candy. "No, never," she answers before taking a bite.

"Is it because I'm so much bigger than you?"

She smirks. "You're really not that much bigger than me."

I almost argue with her, but I decide against it. If my size doesn't bother her, then there's no point in drawing her attention to it. But something set her off, and I need to know what it is so I don't do it again.

She's about to get another candy but changes her mind, folds up the bag, and hands it to me. "Take this from me. They're addicting."

"You can have the whole bag."

She shakes the bag at me. "Take them. I don't need the whole thing."

I take them from her and set it on the table before turning back to her. "So… panic attack… are you feeling better now?" I hate to even say it, but I force the words out. "Do you feel like continuing?"

She seems to think about it, and I'm holding my breath waiting for her answer. "Yeah. I was a little shaky, but the candy helped."

"What do you want to get out of cuddle therapy?"

I caught her off guard with the question. She shrugs and looks down at her hands. "It's all on the intake sheet I filled out."

I nod. "Yeah, but I want to hear it from you. Can you tell me?"

She laughs. "You know, this would be easier if you were ugly."

I sit up a little taller. "You think—"

She interrupts me. "Forget it, I shouldn't say things out loud. I do that a lot without thinking about it. Forgive me."

"Forgiven," I say instantly, even though there's nothing to forgive her for. I appreciate the fact that she finds me handsome, though. It's on the tip of my tongue to tell her she's the most beautiful woman I've ever seen, but I hold back because I feel she's one wrong word from walking out of here.

She leans her head back and groans. "What do I want to get out of cuddle therapy?"

I wait patiently for her to continue, and when she looks at me again, she points to the middle of the room. "Do you care if I pace?"

I sweep my hand out and gesture for her to have at it. "You can do whatever you want, Haven."

She gets up and starts pacing back and forth. Her head is down, and it's obvious she's deep in thought. I'm fine with her taking her time and let my eyes travel down the length of her body. I shift in my seat, making room for my expanding dick. My body has never reacted this way to a woman, not just by looking at her, and I know that the longer I sit here and talk to her, the more my attraction will grow. Maybe a part of me had hoped that once I met her, I would be able to move on and forget about her, but that's not going to be possible. She brings out a protectiveness in me and a need to get to know her better.

"Take your time, Haven. There's no rush," I tell her.

She stops. "I thought the appointment was scheduled for an hour."

"I have nothing to do after this. Seriously, take your time."

It's not quite the truth. I have meetings I was supposed to handle today, but I pushed them back. And I bought every appointment slot for the day to make sure there would not be any interruptions.

She has her hands held together in front of her. "Okay, I want to talk."

I lean forward, resisting the urge to pull her into my lap. "Go ahead. I'm listening."

5

HAVEN

REPEATING HIS QUESTION, I say, "What do I want to get out of cuddle therapy?" I pause, take a deep breath, and hope my face doesn't turn red when I talk about this. In one long ramble, I say everything that is on my mind. "Well, I want to be able to talk about emotions and what I'm feeling without getting sick to my stomach. I want to not freak out when a man reaches for my hand. I want to be able to say 'I love you, too' when my best friend says, 'I love you.' I want to be able to hug someone or let them hug me and not flinch at their touch. I don't want to freak out when I meet someone new and they want to shake my hand. Eventually, I want to let my guard down and let people in."

After my ramble, I look at him, waiting for the judgment or the pity to show on his face, but I don't see it. He tilts his head, scoots farther back in his chair, and crosses his leg over his other one. He looks relaxed, and it causes my stance to soften. I move to the chair I was sitting in and look at him. "You think I'm crazy, right?"

He doesn't smile. "Far from it. All of those are good, Haven, and none of those things you want are unreasonable."

"But—" I start, and he interrupts me. "No buts. You deserve all of that. Hell, you should have anything and everything you want."

Taken aback when he says "hell," I can't hide the surprise on my face. I've been going to therapy for a while now, and I've never had a therapist talk to me the way he is. It's sort of refreshing. I nod my head. "Yeah, I do deserve it. I just need to figure out how to get it."

He starts to reach for me, and I wait for the panic to hit me, but it doesn't. It's more anticipation that I feel than anything. Right before his hand touches me, he jerks it back and mutters, "Sorry." He clears his throat. "As I was saying, you deserve everything you want, and I want to see you get it. I'd like to help you, Haven, if you'll let me."

A calm comes over me, and I nod. "I'd like that."

Before he can ask me anything else, I ask him the one question that I've been thinking about since I first laid eyes on him. It's true that all therapists are different, but I've never seen one that looks like him. He's built like he works out, not like he sits in an office all day. And honestly, he doesn't really talk like any therapist I've been to either. "How did you get into this? Cuddle therapy, I mean."

He shrugs. "Well, it sort of just fell into my lap."

I nod. "Right, I get it. Modeling was the same thing for me."

He leans forward. "Really? Tell me about that."

"I'm originally from Whiskey Run, but after graduating high school, I moved to Jasper to put some distance between my mom and me. I was working at a coffee shop, and someone came in asking me if I'd be interested in modeling. They had a new plus size line they were hoping to promote. I thought it was crazy at first, and way out of my comfort zone, but I was barely able to pay rent. I was living on butter noodles, and I had to force myself to go through with the audition."

"Do you enjoy it?"

"Uh, I guess. It's weird, really because that's the

only time where I feel really confident and in control. It's like a switch turns on and I'm somebody else. It helps me sometimes deal with my 'issues,' but is it my dream job? No, not really. I'll have to figure out something else soon."

"Something else?" he asks. I'm surprised he's not taking notes, but I don't ask him about it.

"Yeah, well, I'll have to retire soon."

"Retire? You're only twenty-five," he says, surprising me. Maybe he has a photographic memory or something because I find it hard to believe that he looked at my intake sheet and just remembered that.

"Twenty-five might as well be sixty when you're talking about modeling."

He looks skeptical. "What are your plans for after?"

I blurt out a laugh. "Uh, I wish I had some."

He smiles indulgently. "Well, what would you like to do?"

"Honestly?" Almost wistfully, I tell him, "I want to be a wife and have kids." I laugh and hold my hand up. "I probably just set women back fifty years by even stating that out loud, but I can't help it. Maybe it's because I didn't have a family—not a real one—when I was growing up. I want people that I belong to… I want people to love me and be able to love them back."

His eyes darken, and he bites his lip. It's almost like he's holding something back.

I laugh, feeling the heat on my cheeks. "Go ahead, laugh. It sounds crazy, I know."

He shakes his head, blinking at me. "It doesn't sound crazy at all."

We're staring at each other, and the connection is intense. I can feel the heat from his gaze from my head to my toes, and I can't stop the tremble of my body.

"Are you cold?" he asks.

I shake my head and stutter, "No. I'm fine." I look at the clock on the wall, and I can't believe that my hour is almost up. The time has flown by. "Uh, it looks like it's time for me to go."

"Wait, uh, can I ask a few more questions?"

"Sure."

I settle back into my seat and wait for him to begin. There are a thousand things I want to ask him, but I don't. For some reason, I have to keep reminding myself that this is therapy instead of a first date or something.

"Are you safe?"

I scrunch my nose up. "Am I safe?"

He clears his throat and nods his head. "Yeah, anyone bothering you?"

I'm not totally understanding the question or why he's asking it, but I answer him honestly. "No one is bothering me."

He smiles and asks his next question. "Okay, and your dad? Is he leaving you alone?" My dad was mostly out of the picture once I got into high school, but he did come see me the first time he saw my picture on a billboard. He seemed to have thought I had money to give him or something, but I'm not sure why King is asking about him.

"I haven't seen my dad in over a year. When he found out I wouldn't give him money, he disappeared again."

His nostrils flare, and almost angrily, he asks, "And boyfriends?"

Surprised, I ask, "Excuse me?"

He sits up a little taller and shrugs as if the question is no big deal. "I'm just curious about the status of your current relationships. It will help me better understand the timeframe and what we're dealing with."

"Okaaaay," I drag out. "Well, I don't have a boyfriend. In fact—geez this is so embarrassing. It's pretty safe to say I've never had a boyfriend."

It's his turn to be surprised. "What? You've never had a boyfriend?"

I let my head drop down and try not to let the embarrassment swallow me up. "It's hard when I don't enjoy being touched by anyone… it just makes it difficult, ya know."

He swallows, hard. "Right… uh, so no one has touched you?"

Without blinking, I stare at him and lick my lips before I answer. "Uh, in high school, I kissed a boy, but no, other than that, I haven't been touched. I don't even let people hug me, King."

He nods, and his breathing has picked up. "Right." He stands up suddenly. "Well, I think that's enough for today."

"Oh… right. You're right. Thanks for staying later with me."

He nods, and I walk over to the door, stopping before opening it. "Thank you, King. I know it sounds crazy, but this was good… this helped me."

He searches my eyes, nodding his head. "When will I see you again?"

"Oh… uh, will Victor be back next week? Or are you stuck with me now?"

He puts his hand to his chest. "I'd like to keep seeing you if that's okay."

I can't stop the smile that forms on my face. *This is not a date. This is not a date,* I keep repeating to myself. "I would like that," I answer him truthfully.

He brings his hand up, and I'm surprised to see he's giving me the orange slices. "Take them. They're for you."

I grab the bag with my left hand, and for the first time ever, I initiate contact and hold out my right hand for him to shake. His eyebrows lift, but he doesn't hesitate. His hand is huge, and he wraps it around mine with ease. I try to commit to memory the feel and the heat of his skin. It feels good, and before I'm ready, he releases his hold on me and asks me gruffly. "When? When can you come again?"

I tilt my head to look up at him. "Victor said twice a week… so I guess next week. I can be here Tuesday."

He nods. "Pick a time."

I look around the room, expecting him to write it in a schedule book or something, but he doesn't reach for one. He doesn't even reach for his phone to put it in. "Uh, I don't know… can you do four?"

"I'll see you Tuesday at four."

I nod, and as I turn to leave, King starts to move with me. I walk into the hallway, and he joins me. Another two steps, and he's right beside me. I laugh. "Where are you going?"

"I'm walking you to your car."

I stop and shake my head. "You don't have to do that."

He reaches for me and then rethinks it, dropping his hands to his side. "I'd like to know you make it to your car safely. I mean, if that's okay with you."

I try to hide my smile as we walk side by side through the hotel and outside to where I'm parked. The whole way, I'm reminding myself, *This is not a date.*

6

———

KING

I'VE BEEN COUNTING down the days and minutes until I get to see Haven again. I've stalked her on social media, researched everything I can find on her, and now I'm pacing back and forth, waiting for her to arrive at her appointment.

As soon as there's a knock on the door, I stride across the room and rip the door open with more force than I should. She jumps at the sudden movement of it, but she's smiling nonetheless.

"Hi," she says with a pretty blush on her cheeks.

It takes everything in me not to reach for her. "Hello, Haven. Come on in."

As she walks in, the server from the hotel restaurant is finishing setting up, and she stands next to the table that is filled with an arrangement of lunch items. "Everything is set up, Mr.——"

I cut her off. "Thank you, Janice. I appreciate you setting things up. We'll let you know if we need anything else."

I pull a hundred dollar bill from my wallet and hand it to her. "Thank you."

She nods, looks at a surprised Haven, and then walks out the door.

"I ordered food. I didn't get to eat lunch, and I thought we could eat while we talked."

"Uh…" She starts staring between me and the table.

I know I've overstepped and this whole thing is unorthodox, but I also know from her social media that she had a shoot today, and she probably missed lunch. I hold my hands up. "No pressure. I saw you had a shoot today and I wasn't sure if you had time to eat."

Her eyes widen in astonishment. "You know I had a shoot today?"

Shit. That doesn't sound appropriate at all coming from what is supposed to be her therapist. "Yeah, I saw it on your social media."

"You looked me up?"

I jut my chin at her, not wanting to deny it. "Yes. Yes, I did."

She waves at the table. "This is… Wow, I mean this is the nicest thing anyone has ever done for me."

Anger rolls through me when she says it. If anyone deserves nice things, it's her. Guilt has been eating at me for lying to her, but I also know that I didn't have much of a choice. At least that's what I keep telling myself.

I pull out a chair for her and gesture to it. "Here. Sit down. I wasn't sure what you'd want to eat, so I got a little bit of everything."

She sits down, and as I move around to the other side of the table and sit down, she's staring at me with her mouth hanging open instead of looking at the food between us. "If you're not hungry… you don't have to eat."

She shakes her head. "No, I mean yes, I am hungry. I guess I'm just surprised is all. This is, while really nice, it's really unexpected, that's all."

I should explain to her, but I'm not sure how she'll react, so that alone has me holding back. "I could tell you why I did this, but I fear it's not appropriate for our working relationship or even something you're ready to hear. Will you eat with me, please?"

She has questions. It's obvious by the way she's looking at me that she wants to understand, but she doesn't ask me anything. She simply nods her head. "I'm starving, King. Thank you for doing this. I thought I was going to have to grab something when I left here."

She reaches for the tongs and picks up a filet steak. "Would you like one?"

I nod, and she puts it on my plate as I tell her, "I should be serving you."

Her smile turns up a notch. "Look at this, King. You did all this. I can surely put food on your plate."

I bind my hands together in my lap as she points at each plate. "Do you like green beans?"

I shrug. "I'll have whatever you don't want."

She laughs and points around the table. "There's enough here for at least ten people."

Without even looking at the food, I tell her, "I'll have whatever you're having then."

She continues to dish up the food, and I don't even pay attention to what she's giving me. I could watch her all night. The way her eyes light up and she smiles as she puts something on my plate. I debated if this was a good idea, but I'm glad I did it because it obviously made her happy.

After she's done serving the food, she holds her fork up. "This is just wow, King. This is so nice of you, and I want you to know how much I appreciate it."

"You're welcome. I'm happy to have a meal with you."

She starts to eat, and I do the same. We're both quiet, enjoying the food, but I can't resist watching her. Whether she realizes it or not, when she likes something, she lets out the tiniest of happy moans. If she takes a second bite, she moans a little louder. I'm enjoying watching her eat so much that I barely even touch my food.

When she notices me staring at her, she lifts her napkin to her mouth and wipes at the corner of her lips. "Do I have it on my face?"

"No."

I can't see her mouth, but her eyes light up. "Why are you staring at me then?"

"Because you're beautiful," I answer without thinking about it.

She folds her arms on the table in front of her. "Wow. Dinner and compliments. You're really pulling out all the stops today."

"I'm sorry… if it's making you uncomfortable…"

My voice trails off as she starts to shake her head.

"No, I get it. I thought about our last appointment all weekend. I know I sounded pitiful… but I don't want you to pity me."

"Pity you? I don't pity you. Why would you think that?"

She looks down at her plate and picks at her food. "It's not a big deal."

I reach for her, and when she tenses, I let my hand fall to the table. "Haven, look at me."

She keeps staring at the table, and I plead with her, "Haven, please."

She finally lifts her big green eyes to me, and I hate the insecurity I see reflected back at me. I can't touch her, so I lean forward, trying to shorten the distance between us. "I promise, I felt a lot of things after our last appointment, but not once did I feel pity for you. I enjoyed talking to you, and even though this is not appropriate, I wanted to sit here with you and do something normal together."

I'm holding my breath, hoping I'm saying the right things, and finally the corner of her mouth lifts, and she nods her head. "Okay. I enjoy talking to you too, King."

There's so much more I want to say, but I hold back because I'm already pushing my luck. We continue to eat, and she tells me about her photoshoot today. She asks me about my day, and I'm vague when I tell her it was busy with appointments, which is not totally a lie. I've had back-to-back appointments, and they would have continued through the day if I didn't cancel them all to be here for this.

"Do you want dessert? I can call Janice and—"

She is shaking her head, putting her hand across her stomach. "No, I can't eat another thing."

I rest my elbows on the table. "Okay. Next question. Do you want to watch a movie?"

I gesture to the corner of the room, where I have the couch and a large screen television set up. She points at herself. "You want to watch a movie with me?"

I nod at her without speaking.

Her brows draw in with confusion on her face, but she doesn't push it. "Okay."

"Comedy, action, or romance?"

I move across the room, and she stands up. "Comedy."

I turn the television on and look at the movies I downloaded earlier. I turn on the first comedy, and Haven starts to clean up the table.

"Stop. Janice will get that later."

She stands up and walks toward me at a slow pace. I can see the hesitancy on her face, and I point at the couch. "Sit down. I can sit next to you or I can sit in one of the chairs. It's up to you. You're the boss here, Haven."

She sits down on the couch and looks up at me. She takes a deep breath, and I know it's hard for her when she says, "You can sit down next to me."

I move slowly because I don't want to spook her, and when I sit down, I make sure that no part of my body touches hers.

I point to the well-known comedy on the television. "Is this okay with you?"

She doesn't look at me as she says, "Yeah, this is funny."

I lean back in my seat and hate that everything has turned awkward. I'm pushing too hard, but I can't help it. There's no doubt I want her, and initially I was drawn to her beauty, but now it's something more. I want to see her smile, I want to see her happy, and I want to see her get everything she wants out of life. It's fast—hell it's all happening too fast, but nothing I do can get her out of my head. I'm constantly thinking about her, worried about her or wondering if she's okay.

There are so many reasons I should walk away from her. One being that I'm fifteen years older than her and another is her lack of experience. I don't want to steamroll her or pressure her in any way. In this instant, I convince myself that I need to slow down.

Before I fuck this up and she doesn't want anything to do with me.

7

HAVEN

THE MOVIE IS ALMOST OVER, and luckily I've seen it a few times or else I wouldn't have a clue what's going on. I have stared at the screen in front of me, but I haven't paid attention. All of my thoughts are on the massive man sitting next to me. About halfway through the movie, he turned his hand palm up on the cushion between us. He hasn't said anything about it, but it's like the elephant in the room because that's all I can think about.

I'm attracted to my cuddler. I shouldn't be, and I'm sure it's against some kind of rule, but I can't help it. I'm not sure how anyone can not fall for his charm. Just being with him makes me feel protected, seen, and heard. It's like his whole focus is on me and what I have to say. Of course, he is paid to do just that.

I have to keep reminding myself that this is not a date… even though it sure feels like one.

"No pressure, Haven."

I'm so lost in my own thoughts I'm not even sure what he's talking about. I turn to look at him, and he's so close. "Huh?"

He doesn't look at me. "No pressure. I can almost hear the wheels turning, and your mind is working in overtime. No pressure, just enjoy the movie."

His hand flexes, and I think about what it would be like if I put my hand in his. Yea, I shook his hand but I imagine this would be different. His hand would be firm but flexible. It would be way bigger than mine, and I wonder what that would feel like. Would it be like a hug for my hand? While all these thoughts whirl in my head, I'm still not saying anything.

He finally looks at me, and I have to suck in a breath the way his eyes are a darker brown and laced with hunger. If I doubted his attraction to me, I don't now. This is more than a therapy session. At least it sure as heck feels like it.

His voice is husky. "I thought we could go slow. My hand is here if you want to hold it."

This can't be natural the way my body reacts to just the thought of holding his hand. It's crazy, but sure enough, my nipples harden, and there's a pull in my lower belly. I whisper back to him, "You want to hold my hand?"

There's humor in his eyes. "Yeah, peaches. I want to hold your hand."

The nickname surprises me, and I want to ask him about it, but I'm thinking too much about the fact I'm about to hold his hand that I can't even begin to process a question to him about it.

I slowly move my hand across the cushion, and when I'm almost touching him, I stop, and all I can do is stare. Don't get me wrong. I want to hold his hand, but just the thought has me freaking out, but not the normal way. At least what's normal for me. I'm not fearful or anxious. I'm not upset about it or wanting to avoid it; it's more of an overwhelming anticipation.

I huff out a breath as my hand trembles next to his. "You think I'm ridiculous, don't you?"

He flexes his fingers, and I can't take my eyes off his strong, long-fingered hand. "Why would I think that?" he asks.

I lick my lips and look at him. "Because it's just holding hands. It's not that big of a deal."

He sounds casual and not the least bit judgmental about it. "To some people it is."

I hesitate, wishing I had the nerve to reach for him. As I sit here and silently debate with myself, he says, "You know, we're not so different, Haven."

"What do you mean?"

"Well, I know you had your mom and dad but not really. Not the way you needed them anyway. I was raised in foster care. Home after home, I made a point of keeping my guard up everywhere I went. I have trust issues, and there are still things that haunt me to this very day."

I put one hand to my chest. "Oh, King. I'm so sorry. I had no idea."

"There were times I wanted to cut myself off from everyone, and I tried that. I was lucky, though. I was thirteen when I was put in a foster home with my four foster brothers and my foster sister. Hell, I feel bad calling them that. They're my family… they are my brothers and sister. If it wasn't for them, I'm not sure what would have happened to me."

I turn to the side, facing him, resting my head on the back of the couch. The movie continues to play, and it's almost over, but it's forgotten as I ask him, "Will you tell me about them?"

He turns toward me, but I notice he leaves his hand open between us. "You really want to hear about them?"

"Of course I do."

He seems to think about it. "Well, I'm the oldest."

I ask without thinking, "How old are you?"

He smirks at me. "Forty."

I nod, quickly doing the calculations in my head. As if I didn't figure it out on my own, he tells me, "I'm fifteen years older than you."

He pauses and then continues. "Holden and Gabriel are brothers. Holden's a baseball player for the Jasper Bears. Gabriel is a firefighter in Whiskey Run. Ledger is in the military, but he's supposed to be retiring soon. Dominic is a mechanic in Whiskey Run, and Chrissy is a nurse at Jasper Hospital, but she lives in Whiskey Run too."

I point to his face. It's something to see the way his face changes when he's talking about his family. "You light up when you talk about them."

The gold specks in his eyes are sparkling. "I love them."

"That's good, King. I'm glad you had them."

His voice is calm and steady. "I got off track. All that is to say that I know what it's like to be afraid to put yourself out there. I know what it feels like when you think the whole world is against you and you're not sure what tomorrow is going to bring… that's all. So yeah, holding hands is a big deal… I know it is, and there's no pressure. I just want you to know I'm here… if you want to try it… I'm here, that's all."

He searches my face and breaks me with what he says next. "I'm sorry no one was there for you, Haven. I'm sorry that you've spent all this time dealing with things on your own. You didn't deserve that."

He lets out an anguished breath, and it's like I can feel how important this is to him. I can't help but wonder if he puts this much effort into all his clients, but a part of me refuses to believe it. I want to feel special to him, even if I'm not.

I'm silent, and he asks, "What are you thinking?"

I look down at his hand that is still open between us. I suck in a deep breath and slowly move my hand to his. We're both staring as I let my fingers slide across his palm and then line them up with his. We sit there for a moment, neither one of us moving.

He's the first to spread his fingers a little, and I let mine slide between until they curl around his. He closes his hand on mine, and I take in the difference between us. His hands are dark, big, and strong. I'm pale in comparison, but it feels good to feel the strength from his touch. I'm the first to move, and I slide my thumb across his. He holds me tighter, and I slowly lift my other hand, placing it on the back of his. King sharply inhales, and I startle my eyes up to his. "Is this okay?"

He croaks, "Yeah, peaches, it's more than okay."

As I stroke my fingers across his hand and then trace his fingers, I ask him, "Why do you call me that?"

"Because I think you're sweet."

I hold on to his hand as a tremble goes through me. A thousand thoughts are going through my head. He's my cuddler. I've hired him to spend time with me. He's older than me and not just a little, but a lot. He's a charmer and knows the right things to say to make me feel comfortable, but I have to remind myself yet again that even though this is all out of the ordinary, it's not real. This is not a date.

And with that thought, I squeeze his hand and then gently pull away. "I should go."

He sighs, and frustration rolls off him, but he doesn't try to talk me out of it. "I'll see you Thursday, then?"

I nod and stand up. "I'll see you Thursday."

I walk toward the door, and he's following me. I could tell him he doesn't have to walk me out, but I know I'd be wasting my breath. We walk side by side, and both our hands are hanging between us. I can't help but imagine what it would be like if we were holding hands like a normal couple. And even though I know it can't happen, I know I'm not going to be able to get it out of my head for the rest of the night.

8

———

KING

I DO my best to blend into the crowd, but I can feel all the eyes on me. My name is well known, but most people don't usually recognize me because I try to stay out of the public eye as much as possible. But there's no avoiding it today.

I had to see Haven.

I set up an alert online so if anything goes public with her name, my phone alerts me. I found out about the fashion show this morning, and it took me about two minutes of debate to decide that I couldn't miss this. I had to see her.

I was at my office, trying to catch up on the last two weeks because my concentration has been on her instead of my work. I was just about to walk out when my brother showed up at the office. I don't get to see him a whole lot, so I brought him with me, and I'm already starting to regret it.

Holden hits his shoulder into mine. "Remind me again what we're doing here."

I'm staring at the stage, and the anticipation builds as I wait to see Haven. "I told you I was busy."

He clasps his hand onto my shoulder and grips hard. "You're always busy, big brother."

I finally look at Holden, and I almost feel guilty until I see the smirk on his face. He likes to bust my balls. "I'm busy? You're the one traveling the country and living your best life."

"I'm working," he explains.

"You play baseball."

He puts his hands on his hips and gives me a death stare. "It's work."

If he can give me shit, I can do the same to him. "Yeah, work, right? You catch a ball."

His voice lowers. "I'm leading the league in putouts. I'm third in the league for homeruns this season… I do more than catch a ball."

"Third? You're slacking, Holden."

"Fuck you," he mutters under his breath.

Finally, I smile, letting him know I'm fucking with him. "Yeah, yeah. I know you work hard. Congratulations on the record, little brother. I never miss a game. But I'm not the one you gotta worry about giving you shit. Gabriel is the one all bent out of shape that you've missed the last three pickleball tournaments. Your brother knows how much you hate to lose, and I'm pretty sure this is the one sport he can beat you at. You have to show up at least one time."

He laughs. "Are you guys still doing that?"

"Yep, once or twice a month. You should really try to join in on the next one. It's actually fun."

He nods. "Yeah, if I'm in town, I'll be there."

Holden is looking around. There are people everywhere, and they're noticing him and taking his picture. Two women have already came up to him and asked for his autograph. He, of course, is eating it up and enjoying the attention. He gets noticed everywhere we go, so I should have known better than to bring him with me when I'm trying to lay low.

"Tell me why we're standing all the way back here. You're King Beckett, Jasper's most eligible bachelor—"

I cut him off. "That was five years ago."

He laughs, "Yeah, well the nickname sticks. There are some seats right in the front. No one is going to ask you to move."

The announcer comes on stage, and thankfully the front row seats that were open only seconds ago are filled up and we're standing in the back row. Music starts to play, and models take turns walking out on stage. The speaker is talking about the clothes, but I completely tune her out and hold my breath until I see Haven walking out onto the catwalk.

I'm completely transfixed on her as she struts across the stage. She has on a bathing suit, and it shows off every one of her luscious curves. My hands fist at my sides because I know there are men in the room drooling over her, and I want to run to the stage and claim her right here and now.

She stops at the end of the stage and kicks her hip out while doing a shimmy from side to side. "Fuck," I groan, and I thought it was low, but the people around me all turn and stare.

I don't care, though. There's no hiding how I feel about Haven. She turns, and then I have a perfect view of her ass as she walks back to the stage and disappears between the curtains. It's only then I look at Holden, and my brother has his mouth hanging open, looking between me and where Haven was just standing. "She's too young for you," he whispers loudly.

All I can do is stare at him. Yeah, I know she's too young for me. She's too everything for me, but I can't stop. I can't stop thinking about her. I can't stop wondering if she's okay. I can't stop wanting her. When I don't answer him, Holden insists, "What are you thinking, King? The news gets wind of this and they will have a field day."

"You act like she's underage or something. I'm not a pervert. She's twenty-five, Holden."

He blows out a breath and pretends to wipe his brow. "Shhhew, well, that's a relief. She's still a little young for you. She's hot, though."

My head jerks, and I glower at him. "Don't even think about it. Brother or not, I'll end you."

He laughs, holding both his hands up. "Whoa, wow! I never thought I'd see the day where the mighty King Beckett would fall in love."

Out of reaction, I'm about to deny it, but I can't bring myself to do it. The show continues, and Haven comes out two more times. Holden finally starts to understand and doesn't try to talk to me when Haven is on the stage. I take her all in. The way she smiles almost shyly to the crowd, the way she moves, the way she flips her hair when she turns. I take my phone out and shoot a video of her as she walks across the stage, and it's about the time that I lower the phone that our eyes meet.

Her smile widens, and there's no doubt she sees me. She's looking right at me.

All I can do is stare at her as my brother, I, and every man in the room fall for her and her absolute beauty.

She walks off the stage, and I nudge my brother. "Come on, let's get out of here."

He doesn't budge, though. "What? What are you talking about? You're not going to talk to her?"

I shake my head and start to push my way through the crowd. Thankfully, because of my size, people move, and I'm able to get out the door without anyone stopping me. The only person that insists on stalling me is my brother. He's followed me, but he's griped about it the whole way outside.

Holden grabs my arm. "King, stop, what's going on? You're obviously into her, why are you not going to stay and talk to her?"

I don't want to tell him, but I need to get it off my chest. I need to tell someone because the guilt is starting to get to me. "She doesn't know who I am."

He looks at me like I've grown two heads. "Well, tell her. It's not like she's going to be upset that a millionaire is attracted to her. Go talk to her."

I mutter shamefully, "She thinks I'm someone else."

He puts his hand up. "What does that even mean? Have you talked to her?"

I nod. "Oh, we've talked."

His forehead creases, and he shakes his head in confusion. "Okay, so who does she think you are?"

Fuck. This is so fucked up. "She thinks I'm a cuddler."

Holden starts to laugh, and when I don't even crack a smile, he stops. "Wait, you're serious? What the fuck is a cuddler?"

I look around at the people walking down the sidewalk around us and then back at my brother. "It's a form of therapy."

He holds his hands up. "Do I even want to know how she came to think you were a therapist?"

I look down at the ground because shame doesn't even begin to cover it. "That's how I introduced myself."

"Fuck, King. What were you thinking?"

"I know. I know. I'm going to fix it."

"You lied to her… fuck, as her therapist. That's

all kinds of fucked up, brother." He rams his hand through his hair and blows out a breath. "All you can do is hope she forgives you when she finds out you're a millionaire."

I give him a dirty look. "She's not like that, Holden."

He shakes his head and walks to where my driver is standing next to my car. "Well, it would be better for you if she was like that."

I jog to catch up with him. "What's that supposed to mean?"

He shakes his head and puts his hands on my shoulders. "It means if she cared about the money, she might forgive you. But if she's a good girl, the kind you'd want to settle down with, then she's not going to be so quick to forgive, King."

Fuck, he's right. I know he's right. I may have just met Haven, but I know her enough to know that she's not going to care about my money. All she's going to care about is the fact that I lied to her. "Fuck, I gotta fix this, Holden."

He puts his arm around me and pulls me to the car. "Yeah, you do. Come on. You promised me food. Let's eat and we'll come up with a plan."

He climbs into the back of my car, and I take one last look at the building we just walked out of.

For just a second, I wonder if I should just go in and come clean, tell her the whole truth and then beg for her forgiveness. But the thought of her walking away from me stops me. I need to prepare because I can't lose Haven… not now… not ever.

9

———

HAVEN

THERE'S a buzz in the room around me. It's always like this after a successful show, and today, the women are even happier than usual. We're all gathered on the stage, and we have to walk back out there and take a bow as soon as the curtain comes up. I'm waiting for it to happen, and when it does, I look at the spot I last saw King. I know it was him. There's no doubt in my mind it was him I saw, staring at me from the back of the room.

But he's no longer standing in that spot. I let my gaze move around the expansive room, but he's nowhere to be found.

The crowd is on their feet, clapping, and after a few waves, smiles, and bows, the curtain comes back down, and we're left backstage.

I move to the dressing rooms, pushing my way through the crowd of models. Everyone else is taking their time, enjoying the high of finishing what was a successful show, and I'm hoping to get ready and possibly catch another glance of King. I know it was him… but why didn't he stick around and say something or at least acknowledge me?

I sit down in front of the mirror to wipe the makeup off my face when I hear one of the other models call into the room. "All right, ladies. Who is it? Which one of you dug your claws into Ridge Beckett?"

Cathy shrills on the other side of me, "I know I saw him in the audience with Holden Gray." I look at her in the mirror, and she's fanning herself like she's trying to cool off.

People keep talking. I hear the words "Most eligible bachelor," "big league player," and "millionaire," but my mind is completely focused on the man that causes me to feel things I've never felt before.

I tune the other models out because I'm not worried about whatever or whoever they're talking about. I'm wondering what King was doing here. It was him, I know it was, and when I smiled at him, he just stared back at me like he was in shock or something. It's okay, though, because I have an appointment with him tomorrow, and I can ask him then.

"Haven, for real, how are you not freaking out? Jasper's most eligible bachelor, a millionaire in the construction industry and super-hot...and he was here in this building. How are you being soooo cool about it all? I mean look at him."

I'm about to swat her phone away when I catch sight of the man on the small screen. Instead of pushing it away, I grab it out of her hands and bring it closer. "That's King," I half-whisper.

Cathy grabs her phone back and makes a big deal of rolling her eyes at me. "His name is Ridge Beckett. I've never heard of King."

I stare in shock at her. That can't be right. King is a therapist... He's not a millionaire or some kind of tycoon. He's a therapist... he's my cuddler. Oh my, did he introduce himself as Ridge at our first session? I grab my purse and bag from under the table I'm sitting at and practically run from the room. As soon as I get outside, I lean against the brick building and pull out my phone. I start searching for Ridge Beckett, and when the first picture comes up, my stomach drops. It's him... Ridge Beckett is my King... my cuddler.

I'm about to read the article with the picture when another model comes out of the building. "Haven, you okay?"

I stuff my phone in my pocket and nod, forcing a smile to my face. "Yeah, yeah, I'm good. Thanks. Good job today, Angel."

She smiles and pulls her bag farther up her shoulder. "Yeah, you too. I'll see you in a few weeks at the shoot for Trends and Treads?"

"Yeah, you know who the photographer is?"

"Axle," she says and rolls her eyes. "Mr. Handsy himself."

"Ugh," I groan. "Okay, well at least we have some time to prepare."

She smiles. "We got each other's back. See you, Haven."

I wave at her, and when she disappears, I start walking down the block toward my small apartment on the east side. I want to stop and finish searching on my phone, but I'm forcing myself to wait until I'm home. The walk seems to take longer than normal, and the whole way, I'm thinking about the betrayal. I have a hundred questions, and I'm hoping that some of them will be answered when I can get online and try to figure this out.

As soon as I walk into my apartment, I slam my

front door, drop my purse and bag, and then pick up my laptop as I sit down on my couch.

As soon as the search window loads, I type in *Ridge Beckett.*

Over a thousand results show up, and I go to the first one. Everything starts to flash in front of me, words jumping out at me. *Millionaire. Most Eligible Bachelor. Construction Tycoon. Ridge Beckett donates fifty thousand dollars to the Children In Need Network. Ridge Beckett attends fundraiser with mystery woman. Is Ridge Beckett ready to settle down?*

I look at the picture with the last headline, and it's him with a blond-haired woman in an embrace. It hits me suddenly, and I feel ill.

Page after page are stories of Ridge Beckett and his business dealings.

I look for anything that will tie him to the cuddler therapist office, and I can't find anything. I know it's a long shot, but there's a part of me still wishing that this was all not a lie. I can't be that naïve… why would a millionaire also be working as a professional cuddler?

When I go to the images tab, I click on the first one, and it shows him with the same beautiful woman on his arm.

It shouldn't bother me, especially now, knowing

he outright betrayed me, but seeing him with other women makes me sick to my stomach, and I'm disappointed in myself because it's jealousy that is raging through my veins. I can't be jealous... I'm mad... not jealous.

I keep going through the pictures. Numerous stories are dedicated to trying to figure out who the woman is. There are so many articles about him and the woman that he is pictured with. Sick to my stomach, I shove the laptop off my lap onto the couch.

He lied to me. Straight-up lied to me.

He's not a therapist, and there's nothing I can find online to tell me otherwise, so he lied to me.

I rest my head in my hands, clenching my eyes closed. I don't know why he did this. What possible reason could there be? Is it a power thing? Was this some kind of bet or something? Even though the proof is right in front of me, I can't help but think this is all a shock. This doesn't seem like the King I know. But what do I know? I fell for the lies. All I know for sure is he lied... and I might never know why.

10

———

KING

"I PASSED!" Victor exclaims as he walks into the office.

I'm waiting for Haven to arrive, and she's already fifteen minutes late. "Congratulations!" I say to him.

"Thank you," he says. "I owe it all to you. I'll pay you back."

I'm shaking my head. "I don't want your money."

He's so excited it takes him a minute to catch on that I'm preoccupied. "What's going on? What time is your"—he holds his hands up to make finger quotes—"appointment?"

"She's late… I think she knows."

Victor's mouth falls open. "Wait, what? She

knows? You mean she knows, knows? Like she knows that you're not a therapist?"

I give one nod, and Victor starts to freak out. "Oh shit, what are we going to do? You're not qualified to do this… oh my God, she's going to sue me… I'll never work in this town again——"

I cut him off. "First of all, you weren't qualified to do this until today, so don't act righteous. Second of all, I'll take care of it."

He sputters and stutters, "You'll take care of it? Why does that sound so ominous? What are you going to do?"

"Fuck, Victor. Chill the fuck out. I'll take care of it."

I may tell him to chill, but I'm freaking the fuck out. She knows. I should never have gone to that show yesterday. I was stupid to think I could go and it wouldn't end up in the paper or something.

I worried all morning that she knew, but when she missed her appointment, I had no doubt something was up.

I could call her, but I need to do this face to face. "Give me her address."

Victor's already shaking his head. "No way, I'm not getting involved. She'll wind up dead or something, and I'll be the one to blame… no way."

I grab on to his collar and shake him. "Shit, man, I'm not going to kill her. I'm going to fix this. Now give me her fuckin' address."

I'm completely on edge and about to lose my shit. He pulls out his phone and opens the appointment app. After some clicking and scrolling, he holds up his phone, showing me her address. I flinch, realizing she lives on the east side in a less than stellar community. Hell, if I knew that, I would have moved her somewhere safer.

Without another word to Victor, I walk out the door, through the hotel, and outside to my waiting driver. "We're going to the east side, Callan."

He just raises his eyebrows and then shuts the door after I get in.

When he's behind the steering wheel, I rattle off the address, and he scrunches up his nose in disgust, but he doesn't say anything else.

When we pull up outside her apartment building, Callan gets out. "Want me to go with you?"

I hold my hand up. "I got this."

I look up and down the sidewalk before walking to the apartment in front of me. There's a welcome mat and a flower next to the door, making it look much brighter and welcoming than the apartments surrounding it.

I knock on the door, and I can hear the sound of shuffling feet on the other side, but the door doesn't open. I knock again. "Haven, I know you're in there. I want to talk."

I wait and am about to knock again when the door swings open. Haven is mad, that much is obvious. Her face is red, and she's glaring at me as she leans against the open door. "Why should I talk to you? I don't owe you anything, Ridge Beckett."

"King," I correct her. "My friends call me King."

She shrugs and glares harder. "Well, I'm not your friend, so I won't be calling you that. What can I do for you, Mr. Beckett?"

I hate the sound of my name on her lips when she says it like that. I frown, but I refuse to give up. That is not an option. "Give me five minutes."

She walks out on the porch and crosses her arms over her chest. "Fine. I'll give you five minutes, but I'll be doing the talking. You lied to me. Why?"

I blow out a breath. "Because I saw you and I wanted to get to know you."

Her lips purse. "So you wanted to fuck me."

I take a step toward her. "I'm not going to deny I'm attracted to you."

She blurts out a laugh. "That's pretty funny that you pick a twenty-five-year-old virgin with intimacy issues. Needless to say, I'm not going to fuck you."

"Quit saying that."

I hate seeing the way she's distanced herself from all this. It's like she's completely cut me off, and I hate it. What I hate more is that I did this to her.

She shrugs her shoulders, and her face is void of any emotion. "Quit saying what? Fuck? That's what it would be, right? You were looking for a quick lay… and you obviously picked the wrong girl, so can we move on now?"

I take another step toward her, and her eyebrows raise, but she doesn't back down. I grit my teeth, wanting to shake sense into her, but I don't touch her. "Quit saying fuck because that's not what we would be doing, peaches. If… when… we do that, it will be making love."

Her mouth falls open, but she catches herself and slams it shut, shaking her head. "Forget it, Mr. Beckett. I'm not falling for anything you say. How did you do this? What happened to my therapist?

Did you off him or something? Is that something you do in your world?"

I slam my hand through my hair. "Why is this the second time today that someone assumes I'm killing someone? I didn't kill anyone. Victor is fine and in the office. I made him do this…"

Her eyes are round and unforgiving. She's shaking her head and tries to walk inside again, but I plead with her. "Haven, stop. Please."

She juts her chin at me, and even though she's trying to be strong, I see the hurt in her eyes. "Was it a bet? One of your buddies want to see you land the fat chick?"

"No. Of course not."

She puts a hand on her hip, and the movement puts her closer to me. "Really? Well, I see the women you date, and I don't look anything like them, so there's something up. Tell me the truth for once. Did you want to see what it was like with a big girl? Is that what this is about?"

I can't hide the anger from my voice. "Quit talking about yourself that way. When I first saw you, I was attracted to you, and I wanted to get to know you. I saw you with Victor, and I didn't even know your fucking name, and I was eaten up with jealousy. Look, I know what I did was wrong. I was going to tell you and then I got to know you—"

She cuts me off angrily. "You don't know me."

"I do know you." I lean down until our faces are only inches apart. "I do know you, Haven. Even though you try to cut yourself off from everyone, you want to feel a connection, like you belong."

She rolls her eyes, and I continue. "You observe people and look for the good in everyone. You're patient and kind, you bite your lip when you're nervous. You're beautiful all the time, and I love to see the confident side of you when you're modeling, but I'm jealous at the same time. You like candied orange slices, you cut your entire steak up before you take one bite, and you prefer to drink water more than anything else." I pause and take a deep breath before I continue. "I know that your family never held you, never hugged you or told you that they loved you. I know I ruined the trust you had in me, but I'm determined to make it right and prove to you that you can trust me and I won't hurt you."

She sucks in and breath and slowly blows it out. "I know that even though you like your job, you want more than anything to have a family of your own."

A lone tear rolls down her cheek, and she wipes

at it angrily. "You know all that because you lied to me about who you are. I thought you were some sort of therapist… and that I could trust you."

I put my hand over my heart as if doing so will hold it together. "You can trust me, peaches."

She shakes her head and takes a step back. "Don't call me that."

When I move to go after her, she puts her hands up to stop me. "No. I don't trust you, Mr. Beckett. As far as I'm concerned, you hurt me, lied to me, and played with me, and now you expect me to just accept it and move on. I can't do that… Forget it, we're just wasting time here… Will you please go?"

"But—" I start, and she stops me.

The tears start to come harder, and it's like a kick in my chest that I can only stand here and watch it. I would give anything to hold her or touch her. "Haven, please."

She moves inside her apartment and puts her hand on the door. "I fell for your lies once, Ridge. I won't do it again."

With that, she shuts the door in my face.

I go to the door to knock again, but as I raise my hand, I can't get the image of her crying out of my head. I hurt her by lying to her, and I've hurt her again by coming today. I know what I need to do even though I don't want to do it. I put my hands on each side of her door and lean my forehead against the hardwood. I need to walk away, but I can't. "Haven… I'm leaving… but I'm not giving up. Just know that I'm not giving up."

There's no response from the other side of the door, so I raise up and shake my head. "I'm not giving up," I whisper before turning around and walking off her porch. Callan has the door open for me, and I slide into the back. I haven't felt this helpless since I was a young kid in a foster home, and I don't like it. But what's fuckin' killing me is that right now, Haven feels worse… and I did that to her.

I WALK into Glaze Bakery with my arms full of flowers. As soon as I get in the door and April sees me, she's shaking her head and pointing at the door. "Oh no. No more flowers." She sweeps her hand around the bakery. "This is a bakery, Haven Weston, and you have it looking like a florist."

Every day since I last saw King, he has had flowers delivered to me, and every day I've been bringing them here when I get my daily dose of caffeine.

I glance around the café, looking through the flowers on every table, and I see Cassie already in a booth, smiling at me. "Fine," I call to April. "Cassie will take them home with her, okay?"

April nods emphatically. "That's just fine, but

don't think you're going to try and leave them behind. I'm already giving out a rose with every purchase."

I try to smile at her. "Well, I'm sure your patrons appreciate that."

She rolls her eyes. "I don't know what's up with what, but maybe you should forgive the guy. He obviously knows he's messed up and is trying to make it right."

I wave at her before dropping down in the seat across from Cassie. I hold the three vases of flowers up. "Here you go. I brought you something."

She leans forward and whispers, "There's no way I can take those home. Baker will not be happy with me bringing home flowers that were sent from another man."

I plead with her, "If you explain, he'll understand."

She laughs. "Baker will not understand, I guarantee it. He's pretty territorial."

I've always been a little jealous of my friend and her husband. It's almost sickening to be around the two of them for how much in love they are. "How come when you say that, it's like you like it that he's territorial?"

She shrugs and smirks. "It's pretty hot, Haven."

I roll my eyes. "Geez, whatever. Fine, you don't have to take the flowers home with you, but you do have to help me dispose of them because I'm not taking them home with me."

"Fine, I can do that."

I lean up and do my best to set them up on top of the table. Cassie reaches over to help me, and we both laugh when we can't see each other because of the huge arrangements. I push them to the side and lean forward. "Thanks for meeting me."

"Of course. How are you doing?"

I lean back and think about the loaded question she just asked me. How am I doing? "Well, I've been better."

She nods and leans forward. "Hear me out."

I tense up. "Okay."

At that moment, April comes over with a tray and sets plates and drinks on the table. "Here you go, ladies. Enjoy!"

"Thank you," Cassie and I say at the same time.

She holds the tray against her stomach. "Okay. Let me know if you all need anything."

"Thanks, April."

She nods and walks away.

Cassie points at the food. "I got you a turkey

sandwich, but we're having dessert today. I don't want to hear any complaints."

I take a bite of the sandwich, and even though I can't taste it, I take my time chewing it up. "Fine."

After wiping my mouth with a napkin, I tell Cassie, "Thanks for meeting me."

She picks at her own sandwich. "You already said that."

I blow out a breath. "Yeah, sorry. I'm not on my game lately."

She nods her head and then leans forward again. "Okay, you going to listen to me?"

I hesitate for just a minute before answering her. Cassie was my best friend in high school, and I'm closer to her than anyone. "Yeah. I'm listening."

"Okay, so I had Baker look into Ridge."

I throw my hands up. "Cassie!"

She shrugs as if it's no big deal. "Please, Baker's a cop, he can do stuff like that, and the fact that this Ridge guy is sending my best friend enough flowers to start her own shop, I should see if he's legit."

I keep quiet and take another bite.

"Did you know he lives in Whiskey Run?"

I shake my head. Hell, I'm finding out that I don't know a lot about Ridge Beckett.

"Yeah, he lives in that huge house that was built out by the lake last year."

"Okay."

"And well, from what you told me, he was telling the truth about his past. He was raised in foster care and aged out of the system."

I try not to let her words affect me, but they do all the same. I have been wondering if he lied about that to me. I keep thinking back to when he told me he was a foster child. It was that story that made me want to hold his hand. Since I've found out who he really is, I've wondered if he told me that sob story because he knew it would break me.

"And…" she starts and then stops.

"And?" I ask her.

"And, well, he obviously regrets what he did."

My mouth falls open. "Cassie, he lied to me."

"I know it doesn't make it right, but why did he lie to you… did you ask him?"

I shrug. Maybe I did ask him, but that whole meeting on the porch is a blur. I barely paid attention to anything after he dropped the little bombshell where he said we wouldn't be fucking, we would be making love.

She leans forward. "Look, I know he did you wrong, but it's been a week. He's called you a hundred times, texted you, sent flowers to you, and all I'm saying is that maybe you should hear him out… that's all."

I set my sandwich down and take a drink of my water. The truth is, he is wearing me down. I have missed talking to him, and I've spent so much time replaying his messages and rereading his texts. I shouldn't forgive him… but maybe I should hear him out.

"Okay," I say.

Cassie's mouth drops open, and she shakes her head. "Okay? Really? There's no way it was that easy… I even left the best for last."

"What do you mean?"

"Remember a few months ago I told you that someone bought that huge empty building across from the elementary and junior high schools?"

I think back, and I do remember that. "Yeah, but no one had any idea who it was or what the building was going to be turned into. Even the planning commission was keeping it hush-hush, and it's crazy that it hasn't hit the Whiskey Run grape vine yet."

She claps her hands excitedly. "Right, well I know." She rolls her eyes. "Well, actually Baker figured it out."

I can already guess, but I ask anyway. "Who is it?"

"Ridge Beckett. The word is he bought it, and he plans to put in a community center for kids."

I sit back in my chair with a thump. This makes it all even more confusing. He can't be that bad of a guy if he's planning something like that. "Well, hell...."

Cassie laughs because she knows exactly what I'm thinking. "See, I told you. Hear him out, Haven. See what he has to say."

I press my lips together and finally give in. "All right. I'll listen to what he has to say."

12

KING

I'M SITTING on Haven's porch waiting for her when I get the text.

"I think we need to talk."

I text her back immediately. "I'm at your apartment. Tell me where you're at and I'll come to you."

Her response is slow, and I'm staring at my phone waiting for her to text back. "I'll be there in ten."

I put the phone in my pocket and then rest my elbows on my knees. I can't see Callan through the tinted windows of my car, but I can imagine the look he's giving me. He's had pity on his face since I fucked everything up last week.

I reread the first text from Haven, and I can't

tell if it's a good text or not. Of course, her finally wanting to talk to me is a good thing, but I'm hoping it's not to tell me to fuck off.

I pat the papers in my pocket, and I hope I'm not about to fuck this up even more. An idea came to me last night. It's crazy, hell, I know it is, but there's no talking me out of it. When I had my attorney draw up the papers, he tried to tell me how crazy it was, but I ignored him and told him to do it.

Ever since then, the more I think about it, the more I want to do it. I'm going to try and not blurt it out to her until I plead my case.

I see her pulling into the parking lot, and I'm on my feet, striding to the driver's side of her car before she's even fully parked. I open her door and then stand back so she can get out.

"Hey, peaches."

She shakes her head, but at least it looks as if she has a little bit of a smile on her face. "Hey."

She walks past me and up the steps of her apartment. I follow behind her and can't help but watch the sway of her hips. As soon as she gets to the door, she unlocks it and walks in. Since she left the door open, I follow her in and stop in the center of the room. She is putting down her purse and bag and then takes a deep breath as she looks at me.

"Thanks for coming."

I put my hands in my pockets so I don't try and reach for her. "I missed you."

She laughs and then sits down on the end of the couch. "Don't talk like that. This conversation is already hard enough."

I sit down on the middle cushion and turn to her. "I want you to know that if you got me here to tell me to leave you alone... I can't."

She tilts her head. "You can't?"

I clasp my hands in my lap. "No, I can't. I think about you all the time, Haven. I know I fucked up... but I need you to let me make it right."

She tilts her head. "Tell me the truth about your family."

"I didn't lie about that. The only lie I told you was being a cuddle therapist. The rest was all true."

Her voice is soft. "So you were a foster child?"

"Yes, and what I told you about my foster brothers and sister... all true."

"Why didn't you just approach me? You're Ridge Beckett."

Every time she says my full name, it guts me. "My friends call me King."

She purses her lips, and when she doesn't say anything, I answer her question. "There are a few reasons I didn't approach you."

"I'm waiting."

She's still angry, but at least she's willing to listen to me. "Because I wanted you to see past my money."

She gasps and puts her hand to her chest. "I don't care about your money."

I put my hand on the couch between us and lean toward her. "I know that now, Haven."

"What else? You said there were a few reasons. What else?"

"When I first saw you, you were with Victor. As soon as you left, I pulled him aside and demanded to know everything about you."

Her eyes are wide. "And he just told you?"

I think back to that day, and I remember grabbing him by his collar. "I was pretty convincing. Anyway, when I found out that he was a cuddler and that you were a client, I knew I couldn't just approach you off the street. I couldn't take the chance that you would tell me no."

She throws her hands up. "So you lied to me."

And I have no other bigger regret. "Yes, I lied to you. And I promise that I'll never do it again."

She searches my face, and there's no doubt she sees the sincerity there. I regret lying to her.

She crosses her arms over her chest. "Do you think you ever would have told me the truth?"

I angle my body toward hers. "Of course I would. What kind of future would we have if you didn't know who I was? I know I messed up, and after I came to your fashion show, I planned to come clean. I was going to tell you at our next appointment."

She tilts her head, and it's obvious she doesn't know whether to believe me or not. It makes me sick to know that I've ruined our relationship. She's going to question everything I say and wonder if I'm telling the truth, but I'm never going to lie to her again. "I'm sorry. I truly am sorry. I know what I did was wrong. I betrayed your trust, and it's going to take me a long time to earn it back, but I want you to know that I'm not giving up. Not on us."

She takes a deep breath and finally nods her head. "Okay, I forgive you."

There's no way it's that easy. "You forgive me? Just like that?"

She smiles, but it's not the big smile I'm used to seeing on her. "I don't hold grudges, King. And you promised you wouldn't lie again."

When she uses my nickname, I start to have some hope that everything is going to be okay. It's not just words that she forgives me; maybe she can actually do it. "I won't lie to you, Haven."

"But…" she starts, and my stomach sinks. "I think it's best if we just stay friends."

I'm shaking my head and insisting, "That's not going to work for me, peaches."

"King, please, it's just—"

I shake my head and scoot closer to her. This would be so much easier if I could touch her. If I could hold her in my arms and show her how I feel about her, but that's not possible. Not yet. All I can do is try and explain and hope she doesn't force me out the door. "I don't want to be your friend… I want to be your husband."

She starts to laugh, but I don't even crack a smile. I'm serious… and somehow I'm going to convince her that she wants to be my wife.

13

HAVEN

I WAIT for him to say, "Ha! Just kidding" or something to that effect. When he sits next to me, looking at me with those big brown eyes of his, almost pleadingly, I shake my head. "You're funny, King."

There's an almost hopeful glint in his eyes. "I'm not joking, peaches. I want you to be my wife."

I jump up from my seat and back away, putting some much-needed distance between us. "Stop that. Stop it right now, King. This isn't funny."

He slowly gets up and follows me. "I'm not trying to be funny. I'm serious."

I shake my head, waving my hands in front of me. "Well, it's crazy talk, and I don't want to hear it."

He comes toward me, and I swear I can't think straight when he's this close. He pulls papers out of his pocket and unfolds them. "Hear me out."

My eyes about pop out of my head. "You had papers drawn up? Are you missing the part where I said we could be friends? I'm not marrying you."

It's almost like the gold flecks of his eyes are sparkling at me. Why does he have to be so handsome? This isn't fair. "You know we can't just be friends. You have to feel this between us, peaches."

I start to stutter. "But... uh... we can't...."

"We can."

I'm still shaking my head, overwhelmed and confused. "But why? Why would we? Why would you want to?"

"Will you sit down?" he asks, pointing at the couch.

I walk over and sit down on the chair, effectively making it so he can't sit next to me, but that doesn't stop him from trying. He sits down in front of me on the coffee table, and the wood groans under his weight.

He has the papers still clenched in his hands. "This is not a joke. I'm not messing with you. I want you to be my wife."

I can barely form a sentence I'm so shocked. "Why?"

He repeats the question. "Why do I want you to be my wife?"

I nod my head, and he leans forward. "Because I'm forty years old. I want to settle down. Hell, you've seen what it's been like since I went to your modeling show."

I blink in confusion. "What do you mean? What's happened?"

He tilts his head. "You don't know?"

"No, I don't. I try to stay off social media." I leave out the part where I spent the whole afternoon searching for information about him when I found out who he was. Since then, I've made a point to stay off the Internet because it was driving me crazy seeing all the pictures of him with that other woman.

He pulls out his phone, scrolls, and then holds it out in front of me. I take the device from him and start reading. *Jasper's most eligible bachelor is on the prowl.* There are articles and pictures about who he was at the show to see. I look up from the phone. "Who were you there to see?"

"Huh?"

"Who were you at the fashion show to see?"

"You, Haven. I was there to see you."

"Oh!" I exclaim.

He puts the paper on the table next to him and then holds his hands out in front of him with his elbows resting on his knees. His hands are palms up, and I know what he wants. He wants me to put my hands in his, but I'm not there yet. "So you want to marry me to avoid gossip?"

"Fuck, no, I'm doing this all wrong. I want to settle down… I want a family. You said you wanted kids—"

Damn. I'm pretty sure my lady parts just exploded. I can't sit across from this hunk of a man and listen to him tell me he wants to have my babies. I'm a strong woman, I know I am, but I'm weak when it comes to resisting King. "I do want kids, but this was not the way I thought it would happen. Contracts and—"

He grabs the papers and holds them up. "If you don't want a contract, I can rip it up. But I was trying to protect you too."

He shoves his hand through his hair and looks at me wildly. I'm not sure what is going on in his head, but it's obvious that he's thought about it, and he's determined to make it happen.

"Let's talk about this. You want a kid? Why get

married? This is the twenty-first century, after all. If we wanted to have a child… we could just have a child." Where did this even come from? I'm not having a kid with him. Why am I humoring him by even talking about it?

"I would want the baby to have my name."

I scrunch up my nose. "You know you can do that without a wedding, right?"

"That's the deal, Haven. Marriage. Kids. The contract has it all in there. If you decided to end the marriage, I would still take care of you and the kids."

Speechless, I stare at the papers in his hands. He tries to give them to me, but I'm not taking them. "Why would you do this?"

"I like you. I trust you. I want a child. You said you want one too."

I laugh out loud. He makes it sound so simple, and it's crazy. "I can't marry you to have a child, King. Yes, I want a baby, but I want more than that. I want a real marriage. I want a man that loves me and will be faithful."

"I will be faithful," he exclaims, but I can't help but notice that there's no professing his love for me or anything.

"I'm sorry. I can't."

His jaw tightens. "I'm not taking no for an answer, peaches."

And I believe him when he says it. "Fine. I'll think about it."

He doesn't like that answer either, but at least he doesn't insist on a yes right now. With his hands palm up in front of me, he asks, "Do you think you could ever be comfortable with me?"

I should tell him no. I could end this all right now if I told him I felt nothing when I look at him and that I don't want his hands on me. But it would be a lie.

"Honestly?" I ask him.

He looks shamed but nods. "Yeah, I know I don't deserve it, but yeah, I want the truth."

I let out a long breath. "You make me feel alive, King. More alive than I've ever felt in my life… and that freaks me out."

He clears his throat. "Me too, peaches."

I can see the sincerity in his eyes, and I gently put my hands in his.

He holds on to them, and his voice is thick with emotion. "I want to try something."

I bite my lip as my stomach churns with nervousness. He's already shocked me with the fake marriage request… I can't imagine what's going to come out of his mouth next. "What?"

"Can I hug you?"

My voice drops to a whisper. "Hug me?"

"Hug you," he repeats.

Shakily, I nod my head, but secretly, I'm waiting for the panic to set in.

He stands up and pulls me up with him. We're standing chest to chest, and I can feel him move with every breath he takes. All my senses are alert, and I have to remind myself to breathe.

"Give me a safeword."

Heat creeps up my neck and face. "A safeword?"

"Yeah. If you get overwhelmed, then just say it and I'll stop. I'll let you go."

"Pickles," I blurt out. "I don't like pickles."

He smiles and brushes a strand of hair off my face and pushes it behind my ear. "Okay, one more thing I can add to the list of things I know about you. You don't like pickles, so just say pickles if you want me to let you go."

Okay, I mouth because no sound comes out.

Very slowly, he lets go of one hand and brings it up my arm, over my shoulder and to my back. He's searching my eyes the whole time, and I'm sure he's afraid I'm going to have another panic attack. I give him a slight nod, and he releases my other hand and does the same until both of his arms are around me. When he has me securely against his chest, his body shudders, and he pulls me closer.

"Are you okay?" he asks, his lips right next to my ear.

"Yeah," I admit with a pleasure-filled voice.

"Put your arms around my waist, Haven. I want to feel you hug me too."

I realize that I'm standing here in his embrace with my arms hanging at my sides. Slowly, I let my hands come up to his waist, and I tentatively touch him there. He sucks in a breath, and I lean back to look at him. "You okay?"

He nods. "Yeah, don't stop."

I slide my hands around him until I'm pressed against him and I'm holding on to his back. I can feel his muscles move everywhere I touch him, and we stand here in each other's arms without saying anything. He rests his cheek on the top of my head and holds me flush against his hard body. It feels so good, and I don't want it to end.

"You feel good in my arms, peaches."

I lean my cheek against his chest, and I can feel his heart beating wildly. "This feels good, King."

I should probably be embarrassed. I know he's way more experienced than me and that I'm making a big deal over a hug, but this feels good… it feels right. "I've never been hugged before."

"Never?" he asks huskily.

I try to think back, and I can't remember ever being in someone's arms… not like this. "If I have, I was too young to remember it."

His hand comes up and cradles my head against him. "Maybe we can do this more often then because I can already tell this is going to be an addiction for me."

I sigh and lean into his touch. "Me too," I whisper.

14

———

KING

SHE DIDN'T SAY NO. That's what I have to keep reminding myself.

It's been two days since I last saw Haven. I've texted her every morning and every night, not to pressure her but just to connect with her. She's texted me back, but she's completely avoided the topic of marriage.

That day in her apartment keeps replaying in my head. How do I feel more from one hug than I've ever felt about anything else? I need to convince her to do this with me, but I'm not sure how.

"Spill it, King. Why did you bring us all here?"

My brothers bring me out of my thoughts. I invited them over to the house after we played our monthly tournament of pickleball. Gabriel won yet again, and as they've been talking smack, I've been lost in thought trying to figure out what I need to say.

My brothers Dominic and Gabriel are fighting over the last piece of pizza, and I laugh at their antics. When Dom comes up with the last piece, he takes a big bite and says, "Yeah, spill it, King. You got beat tonight, and I didn't get to enjoy it half as much because I don't even think you realized you lost."

I set my plate down and lean back in my chair. "I'm getting married," I blurt out.

They both start to talk at once.

"Married?"

"Don't do it."

"I knew something was up."

"To who?"

"When do we meet her?"

Thank goodness Holden is playing baseball down south because I really don't need him here telling the story of how Haven and I met. I try to answer their questions. "Yes, married. Her name is Haven Weston."

Gabe leans over and fist-bumps me. "When's the wedding? And when do we get to meet her?"

Shit. Here's the sticky part. "Well, she hasn't actually agreed to marry me yet."

Both their mouths drop open.

I hold my hands up. "I know, I know. Listen, I may as well tell you because Holden's not going to let me live this shit down." I go through how I met Haven, and I'm getting glares from the both of them. They don't like it. We were raised rough, and it brought out an honesty in all of us. We don't always do the right things, but I know what I did was low. "I fucked up big time. She says she forgives me, but so far, she's not agreeing to marry me."

Gabe throws his hands up. "Can you blame her? You lied to her."

I'm still ashamed of how I handled this. "I know…. But I'm going to make it right."

Gabe rubs at the scruff of his beard. "So explain it to me. Are you marrying her because you love her… or because you're trying to make this right?"

Love. Just hearing that word makes me want to sink into myself. What have I got from love? Nothing, and I'm not ready to open my heart to it just yet. "I'm not marrying her because I want to make it right… I'm marrying her because I can't stop thinking about her… because I want to have a family… a wife… a child."

Dom is shaking his head. "Well, I don't know many women that are going to get married without love, King."

I shrug my shoulders. "She knows the deal. I explained the contract to her."

"Fuck." Dom groans. "Really? You drew up a fuckin' contract? You really don't know anything about women, do you?"

"King!" Gabe exclaims. "Are you ever going to learn?"

I hold my hands up because I had hoped my brothers were going to be able to help me, but I should have known they were going to bust my balls over this. Maybe if Ledger was here, he would be on my side. He's even more strategic and less emotional than me. He would get it. He's retiring from the military soon, and I'm ready for him to come home. I've missed him.

Hell, even Holden would try to help. But these two are too busy telling me all the things I've done wrong instead of trying to give me any kind of tips on the matter. "Look, guys, you don't know her. She had a rough upbringing, and she's fine with this."

But even as I say the words, I wonder if I'm

telling the truth. It sounds ridiculous saying it out loud, even to me. Wanting to change the subject, I pick up the empty beer bottles to take to the trash. "Forget it, guys. You'll meet her soon; I'll make sure of it."

"But—" Dom starts, but I interrupt him. "Forget it. I know I fucked up, and I'll figure out how to make it right."

I walk out of the living room and drop the bottles into the trash, and when I walk back in, Dom continues like I never left. He leans forward. "Well, the first thing you need to do is rip up the fuckin' contract."

"I had the contract written up so she'd know I would always take care of her when it ended."

Gabe smacks his hand to his head. "When it ended? You're not even married and you're planning for it to end?"

I sit up a little taller and try to keep my voice void of emotion. "Yeah, well, love doesn't last. We all know that."

They both just stare at me, not knowing what to say. I know it sounds shitty, but I've had a lifetime of sad endings, and I'm just trying to keep it real. Finally, the guys are speechless. I don't think they can argue with me on this.

"Let's change the subject. What do you guys know about the guy Chrissy's out with?"

Our foster sister is the youngest of all of us. We have all looked out for her through the years, and we're all pretty protective of her.

Gabe hits his hand on the table. "What the fuck? Chrissy's out on a date? I don't know anything about that."

Dominic shrugs. "I don't know. She won't tell me anything about him."

It's my turn to roll my eyes at them. "Well, no shit. Why would she tell you two anything? The last date she was on, you two crashed it and sat right behind them at the movies."

Gabriel gets up. "I don't like it. I'm going to check on her."

Before either Dom and I can say anything, Gabe is out the door. Dom looks at me. "What's that about?"

I start cleaning up the pizza boxes. "You know how he is about Chrissy. They've always been close."

Dom looks at the door Gabe just walked out of and then at me. "What are you going to do? About your future wife, I mean?"

"I'm going to convince her to say yes… There's no other option, Dom."

He stands up and crosses his arms over his chest. "I don't know, man. I know you don't know much about it, but the way you talk about her… the way you look when you talk about her… I think there's more to it than some kind of contract, fake marriage kind of bullshit you seem to claim it is."

I'm not going to argue with him because maybe, just maybe, he's right.

15

HAVEN

I'M a nervous wreck by the time I walk into his office a few days later.

I've thought about it, and I've done the thing where you write all the pros and cons, and I even told myself that I'm going to tell him no. That was the plan. But as I walk into his office building, doubt creeps in.

There are so many things that scare me, but one of the biggest things is that I'll never feel the way I feel when I'm with King.

And that right there is enough for me to say yes to his crazy idea.

I walk to the front desk, and the woman smiles at me. "Hello. How can I help you?"

"Hi. I'm here to see King... I mean, Ridge Beckett if he's not busy."

The smile on her face freezes. "I'm sorry. Mr. Beckett is in a meeting. Can I give him a message?"

I hesitate before giving her my name, but I figure I might as well do it. "Yeah, uh, can you just let him know I stopped by? I'm Haven Weston."

The woman jumps up. "Haven, it's so nice to meet you. I'm Rachel Raymond, and I'm Ridge's assistant. Hold on and I'll grab him."

I hold my hands up and start to back away from her desk. "Oh no, I don't want to disturb him. I can call him later."

She comes around the desk. "No, please don't go. Ridge said if you came by to make sure I interrupt whatever he's doing and not to let you leave. Come on, I'll take you to his office and then I'll let him know you're here."

I follow behind her in shock. I'm not sure what I expected, but it wasn't this. As soon as she leaves me in his office, I look around the big room with the dark mahogany desk and bookshelves. It's definitely a step up from the barren office at the cuddler offices. I walk over to the window and look out at downtown Jasper.

When the door opens, I turn on my heel, and

King is standing in the doorway, smiling at me. "You came."

My mouth drops seeing him in a suit. The man I've seen has been in dress shirts and khakis or T-shirts and jeans. He's built like a man that works with his hands, but this side of him is just as sexy, and I can't help but stare back at him.

"Haven? Are you okay?"

I finally pull myself together and gesture to the door behind him. "It seems to me you expected me since you told your assistant to make sure I stayed."

He walks into the room with his hands in his pockets. "It was wishful thinking on my part."

He walks over to me, and my heart stutters as he approaches. "You know what I've been thinking about?"

I wonder if it's the same thing I've been thinking about. "What?"

He holds his hands out, palms up. "That hug."

I look at his outstretched hands, and there's no denying him. I put my hands in his, and just as soon as I do, he pulls me into him, wrapping his arms around me. I melt into him, wrapping my arms around his waist and resting my head against his chest. "I've thought about this too."

He takes a deep breath and lets it out slowly. "Tell me your answer… tell me yes, peaches."

I sigh, wanting him to have an out. "Are you sure you want to do this?"

"Yes," he answers without hesitation.

"And you know we can have a baby without getting married?"

"It's non-negotiable, Haven."

I thought about this all night and how I was going to approach the subject. He wants a kid, he's made that known, but he didn't really say how we were going to get there. I'm guessing artificial insemination, but I need to clarify that with him. It makes it easier that I'm leaning against him and he can't see my face. "So I'll be a pregnant virgin?"

He leans back, keeping his hands on me, but he searches my eyes. With a smirk, he asks, "Did you think you would get pregnant in a doctor's office or something?"

Heat rushes to my face. "I assumed that's what—"

He leans down until I can feel his hot breath on my cheek. "We'll be getting pregnant the old-fashioned way, Haven."

I swallow hard as my whole body reacts and

gets hot. I feel like I need to fan myself, but I stand perfectly still. "I'm still going to work."

He doesn't seem fazed by my request. "I'm not going to try and control you. You can have the life you want."

I suck in a breath. "I want a small wedding. Just us."

Again, he doesn't hesitate. "Whatever you want."

"The contract needs to be changed. I don't want your money. If you want to provide for any child we may have, that's fine, but I want my name taken off of it."

"No, that's not part of the deal."

I pull back, out of his reach, to put some distance between us. "It's important to me, King. You will always think I agreed to this—hell, whatever this is—a fake marriage because I wanted your money, and that is not the case."

"Why are you doing it?"

I lift my head and look straight into his eyes. "Because I'm comfortable with you, well, more comfortable than I've ever been with anyone, and I want to have kids. This is my chance—hell, it could be my only chance."

He nods. "I'll have the contract reworded, but

just so you know, peaches, I will always take care of you."

I figure it's best to change the subject. "Where will we live? Will we live together?"

"Yes, of course, we will. To anyone else this is real. We will live at my house… in Whiskey Run. If we ever need to stay in the city, I have an apartment in Jasper, too."

"Are you going to see other women?"

He reaches for me, putting his hands on my shoulders. I didn't realize how worried I was about it until he starts shaking his head. "No, I wouldn't do that to you. Plus, I haven't looked at another woman since I first saw you. I'm consumed by you."

My heart starts to race. This is embarrassing to talk about, but it's important to get it out there. "What if we do this… what if we get married… and I can't, you know, perform?"

He tilts his head and smiles. "I can wait."

"What if I have another panic attack?"

His forehead creases. "That scared the hell out of me the first time, but I'll stick by you, Haven. I'll talk you through it just like last time."

"Are we working on some kind of timeframe or anything like that?"

He shrugs, and it's killing me how easygoing he

is about this. "I want us married soon. Everything else—there's no pressure."

I lift my head, searching his eyes. I'm still not sure about any of this or if I'm making the right decision, but I know if I told him no, I'd regret it for the rest of my life. "And how long do you plan for us to stay married?"

I hold my breath, trying not to let any disappointment show. I keep telling myself I can do this. It's a part I'm playing—it's not real, but I'm not sure if my heart is planning on playing along. He shakes his head. "Let's not put an end date on it."

Finally, when I feel like I've got all the answers I wanted, I nod my head. "Okay."

His hands tighten on my shoulders. "No more questions or requests?"

I lick my dry lips and nod. "Yeah, just one."

His hands cup up on each side of my neck, and he holds me there. It doesn't slide by me that he's touching me and I'm not freaking out. As a matter of fact, he's gone out of his way to touch me the whole time I've been here. It's almost like he's trying to get me accustomed to his touch.

"Anything," he says.

I look into his eyes and force the words out. "I think before we do this, we should kiss."

He leans in, and his voice is husky. "You want me to kiss you?"

I wet my dry lips and nod. "Yeah, I mean just to be sure the chemistry is there."

His hand tangles in my hair, and he holds the base of my neck. He's looking at me with a small smirk. "You don't know if we have chemistry?"

I put my hands on his chest and slide them up to his shoulders. "Well, I mean, I know how I feel just when you touch me, but I didn't know if you wanted to kiss me to make sure you were really attracted to me, that's all." I blow out a breath, a little embarrassed. "I just thought before we did this, you'd at least like to…"

I trail off because I've said too much. I sound like a desperate fiend, begging him to kiss me or something. I just thought before we did this we should at least kiss.

He lifts my chin so I have no choice but to look at him. "I don't have to kiss you to know I'm attracted to you. I've held back because I don't want to freak you out, but we should be upfront about this. I want you, peaches. I want you more than I've wanted anything in my life. When I hold you, I have to will my body not to react." He leans down, and I can feel his breath on my cheek. "The chemistry is there, and it's undeniable."

My breath is stilted, and I'm not sure what to do. I'm dying for him to kiss me, but I've already asked him for that, so now it's up to him.

"I'm going to kiss you now."

As soon as he says it, his lips are on mine. He starts slowly, with a soft kiss on my lips. It feels good, but it's not enough. My eyes close, and my fingers grip the material of his jacket, afraid he's going to stop. I'm not sure what I'm doing, but I know I want more.

He leans back and looks at me. "Are you okay?"

It comes out as a growl, and my eyes jerk to his. "Yeah, yeah, I'm okay."

"I want more."

I nod, and then he's on me, sealing his mouth to mine. He tilts my head to the side and possesses my mouth in a kiss that has my whole body reeling. His hands go to my back, pulling me flush against his body as he kisses me until I'm breathless.

My knees feel like jelly, my heart is racing, and there are goosebumps on my arms. The reaction is overwhelming, but all I can think is *Don't stop. Please don't stop.*

When his tongue sweeps along mine, there's no holding back the moan. He takes full advantage, deepening the kiss, and my tongue meets his.

His hands go down my back, and he cups my ass, pulling my lower body against his. There's no denying his arousal as it digs into my belly. I pull back, gasping, but he doesn't let me go. "Okay?"

I nod, and I'm sure my eyes are as round as saucers. "Yes… wow… I never…"

Before I can get the rest out, he rests his forehead against mine and whispers raggedly, "Me either… not like that."

I close my eyes and try to catch my breath, wondering what I've gotten myself into and if my heart is going to survive it.

16

KING

IF SOMEONE WOULD HAVE TOLD me that I'd be at a fashion show twice in two weeks, I wouldn't have believed them. But today, there's nothing that could keep me away from here. It's been a few days since Haven agreed to marry me, and now I'm doing my best to wear her down on setting a date. Since she agreed, it's made me a crazy person, and I want anyone and everyone to know she's mine.

There's a fundraiser that I have to attend tonight, so my sister, Chrissy, and I are here for Haven's show, and then the three of us will be going to the fundraiser together.

"Oooh, first row... fancy. Remind me to go places with you more often." Chrissy preens sitting next to me. She's looking at everything in awe. We're already halfway through the show, and my eyes are focused on the stage, waiting to see Haven.

"Enjoy it. Haven should be out soon." As we're waiting for Haven to come out, I lean over and whisper, "How'd your date go the other night?"

She rolls her eyes. "Great, until Gabe showed up at the Whistler and sat down between us. He's taking this big brother, best friend thing a little too far. Geez, anyone I try to date gets the third degree."

I agree that Gabe takes it a little too far sometimes, but I'm still going to have his back on this one. "You can't be mad. You're our little sister… we have to look out for you. It's like a rule or something."

"I'm thirty-three years old, King. I think I can handle a date in downtown Whiskey Run. I mean, come on, everyone knows you guys, and most guys are too scared to even date me. I have to say yes to the ones that actually have the guts to ask."

I look at her skeptically. "But do you?"

She is frustrated, but she changes the subject. "I can't believe you're getting married… and to someone I haven't even met."

For the first time, I turn my attention to Chrissy.

I hate to think I've hurt her feelings. Everything has happened so fast, but I'm not slowing it down. That's why I invited Chrissy to tag along with us tonight. "You're going to love her, sis."

She turns her full body to the side to look at me. "Oh, I'm sure I will. How about you? Do you love her?"

I lock gazes with her, and I don't have to explain my past or who I am. Chrissy is seven years younger than me, but she knows what we all went through. "I'm incapable of love."

I turn to look at the stage, and Haven is walking straight to us. She's smiling, but it's not the smile I'm used to, and she looks between Chrissy and me before turning and walking back the way she came.

I'm not sure why, but I feel unsettled.

As she disappears off stage, Chrissy leans into me. "I don't think you're as incapable of love as you think you are."

I don't answer her because I can't. I'm not sure what this feeling is because it's all new to me. The obsession I have for her, the jealousy, the possession that haunts me when I think of her tells me that I'm feeling more for her than I've ever felt before. "Come on. Let's go."

Chrissy stands up. "Go? What about Haven?"

"We're going to get her."

As soon as I make the decision, I'm leading Chrissy toward the back of the room. I'm not sure if I can get backstage, but I need to see her. I am familiar with the look I saw on her face because I felt the same way when I saw her with Victor the first time.

As we get backstage, there's a hush in the room, and then everyone starts talking at once. A woman that is scantily clad walks up to me. "Ridge Beckett, I'm Cathy. Thank you so much for coming to the show."

I nod and angle my body to get past her without touching her and then I don't stop until I get to where Haven is standing. She's still looking between Chrissy and me, and I realize now I should have told her I was bringing my sister. I hold my hand palm up in front of her, and she looks at it in surprise. It's like I'm holding my breath until she puts her hand in mine. "Haven, you're beautiful." I lean in and whisper in her ear, "She's my sister. You have nothing to be jealous of."

She blushes, and her eyes light up. I pull her against my side. "Haven, this is my sister, Chrissy. Chrissy this is Haven, my fiancée."

Haven gasps when I introduce her as my fiancée, but I can't ask her about it because Chrissy squeals excitedly. Thankfully, I've already told her about Haven's aversion to touch, and she doesn't reach for her. She gives her a little wave. "Haven, it's so good to finally meet you."

She nods her head. "It's so good to meet you too. King has told me so much about you."

"This is so amazing. I'm so over being the only girl, and I'm excited to finally have a sister."

An emotion like I've never seen comes over Haven, and she murmurs, "Me too."

I pull Haven into my chest, wanting to soothe her, and whisper against her ear, "Get dressed, peaches, so we can get to the party."

She nods against my chest. "Okay. I'll be ready in five minutes."

"No rush."

Chrissy is looking between us, and Haven smiles shyly at her. "You want to hang out here with me to get ready?"

Chrissy nods, and I leave the two of them with the promise I'll be waiting for them. As soon as I walk out the door, cameras are going off, but I ignore them and stand off to the side. The flash of the bulbs is annoying, but I've learned that if I engage, it escalates quickly. So I pull out my phone and start returning emails that I've been ignoring.

Hardly any time at all goes by, and Haven and Chrissy are walking out laughing together. "That was fast."

"I told you it would only take five minutes." She turns side to side. "Do I look okay? I brought three dresses, but Chrissy and I thought this one was the best for tonight."

I take the bag off her shoulder and put it over mine, and then I take her hand, bringing it up to my lips. I want to kiss her, but right now, this is the best I can do. I'm not sure how she'd react if I do what I want to do and kiss her lips instead. The flash bulbs are going off all around us, but I tune them all out because I'm one hundred percent focused on Haven. "You look stunning."

She blushes and leans in. "Uh, King, we're putting on a show."

"Does it bother you? Being seen with me?"

She laughs, slapping her hand against my chest and tries to play it off, but something in my face makes her somber. "No, of course not. I couldn't be prouder than to be seen with you."

I bring her against me and whisper into her ear, "I wish we were alone."

Chrissy snickers and leans in. "Well, you're not. Now let's get out of here. You two have the rest of your lives to be all sappy with each other. I'm ready to mingle."

17

―――――

HAVEN

I KNEW this was a bad idea.

I've been here for less than an hour, and it's overwhelming the number of people that are here. The last thing I want to do is embarrass myself or King, but it may be unavoidable if this woman doesn't back the fuck off.

I'm not sure how I ended up in this situation. One minute I was standing with King and Chrissy and the next, King got called away to meet with someone who wanted to speak with him, and then Chrissy went to the bar to get a drink. As soon as they left, these three women approached me, and they're asking one question after another.

"I attended the women's summit conference a few months ago. You were a speaker."

I nod and smile, but the look on the woman's face has me keeping my guard up. "Yeah, that was me."

She crosses her arms over her chest. "You gave a speech on body positivity and self-confidence."

I look around the room, hoping to spot King or Chrissy, but neither of them are in sight. I suck in a breath, wondering where this conversation is going. "That's right, I did. Did you enjoy the conference?"

The woman tilts her head back and looks down her nose at me. "I just think it's very irresponsible of you."

"Excuse me?"

She waits for someone to walk by, smiles at them with an innocent look, and then sneers when she looks back at me. "I said I think it's very irresponsible of you to talk about things such as health. I mean, all you're doing is promoting an unhealthy lifestyle."

I put my hand on my hip. "I'm sorry, I don't think you're talking about my segment because I talked about the importance of nutrition and how you can be beautiful regardless of your height, weight, hair color, skin color, and everything else that people judge us on."

She gestures up and down my body. "But you're fat."

I gasp, and the other two women at least seemed to be embarrassed by their friend's outburst. I do my best not to react because I'm sure that's what she wants. "Yes, I'm plus size."

The woman opens her mouth, and at that moment, Chrissy comes up, threading her arm through mine. Normally, I'd react poorly to the attention, but right now, I'm appreciating the gesture. "Karen, hi, I see you've met my future sister-in-law."

The woman looks at Chrissy. "Oh…" She looks me up and down. "And which brother is she marrying?"

"Well, Ridge, of course."

The woman gasps, and Chrissy's smile widens as she turns to me. "As a matter of fact, I'm sure King is looking for you now. Let's go find him."

We start to walk away, but I stop because I know I'll be upset with myself if I don't say something. I've always had to stand up for myself and I'm not going to stop now. "Karen, right? That's your name?"

Still in shock, the woman nods. I've noticed that we have seemed to draw a crowd, and I hate it, but I can't walk away without saying something. "Well, I may be bigger than average, but that doesn't mean I don't have worth. I don't know who was mean to you or made you this way, but I hope you know that you can be better than this... you can do better. We should be taking care of each other... not tearing each other down."

I wait for her to respond, but I get nothing. I guess there's no changing people. "Have a good night," I mutter before turning with my future sister-in-law. She is staring at me with her mouth wide open. "I can't believe you just..."

I visibly start to tremble. I hate confrontation, and I'm usually good at avoiding it. Chrissy stops talking and quietly walks beside me toward the opposite side of the room. We don't stop until we're standing in the corner. Somewhere along the way, she picked up two glasses of wine and hands one to me. "Here. Drink up."

I take it from her and take a sip. I'm expecting to have people watching me, but I can't see any of them because King comes to stand right in front of me. "What's wrong? What happened?"

Chrissy throws a hand up. "Karen Reynolds happened! She's such a bitch," she seethes.

King reaches for me. "What did she say to you?"

"I'm fine. I shouldn't have said anything. I'm sorry if it comes—"

Chrissy interrupts me. "Don't even finish that sentence. King would not expect you to let someone talk to you the way she did. You handled it great and with such class, Haven. I was impressed. I get mad, and I start crying and get hysterical… You were calm and put her in her place."

I take another sip of the wine, and then Chrissy nudges her brother. "I'm going to give you all a minute. I'll be over there if you need me."

I see the look Chrissy gives King, and I'm literally sick over all this. "This is a bad idea, King," I tell him as soon as his sister walks away.

"What do you mean, this is a bad idea?"

"I mean I'm not cut out for this. I'm not into these social parties and—"

"This charity is important to me, Haven, and I attend every year. But this is not something I do every week. Two or three times a year, I'm expected to make an appearance."

My stomach does a little flip. It soothes my heart to know that feeding hungry children is important to him. I don't want him to think that's my problem because it's not. "I understand that, King, and I love your giving heart, but what I'm saying is that people are shocked when they find out I'm your fiancée." I gasp, and my hand goes to my mouth. "Oh my God, Chrissy told them we're engaged. Everyone is going to know."

"Good."

I grab on to his wrist. "No, you don't understand, people—"

He cuts me off. "The only people I care about is you, peaches."

I search his eyes and see the sincerity on his face, but I still feel uneasy. I can feel the people watching us and no doubt talking. "Maybe we should put off the wedding… I just caused a scene, and maybe we should see if it blows over… maybe…."

I stop and blow out a breath, overwhelmed by it all.

"Marry me tonight, Haven."

"Tonight?" I exclaim.

He nods and puts his hand over his chest pocket. "I've been carrying around your rings. I wanted you to be wearing it when we got here tonight, but I didn't think you'd appreciate me asking you with my sister and an audience."

I tilt my head back to look at him. "You should think about this."

"There's nothing to think about. I want you to be my wife."

I don't know what to think about any of this. The night has been a roller coaster of emotions. First seeing him with Chrissy and the jealousy that raged inside me. It was Chrissy in all the pictures with him. It was his sister that I was jealous of and have been stewing about. Then him coming backstage and automatically knowing how I'm feeling and putting me at ease. The way he's held my hand or touched me all night is making me want all kinds of things.

He crowds against me. "I'm sorry for leaving you… I shouldn't have."

"I can take care of myself, King. It's not your job—"

"You don't have to take care of yourself anymore. I know you can, I know you're self-sufficient and you don't need me, but I still want to be the one that's there for you."

I lean into him. "How can I say no to that, King?"

He leans down and whispers to me, "I hope you can't, Haven. Be my wife."

Oh God, there's something about the way he says my name. "Okay."

His eyebrows raise. "Okay? You'll marry me?"

I go up on my tiptoes to whisper to him, "If you're sure."

He doesn't wait to seal the deal. He puts his hands on each side of my face and leans down to kiss me. This is all going so fast, but it feels right. When he pulls away, he takes out his phone. "We'll give Callan your key; he's going to grab some of your clothes."

"But why?"

He smiles and pulls me to his chest. "Because we're getting married tonight."

"Tonight? But how?"

He anchors his hand around my neck and leans down, pressing his forehead to mine. "Let me take care of it."

There's no way I can tell him no. "Okay…"

He kisses me again and then starts making phone calls.

18

___

KING

EVERYTHING COMES TOGETHER EASILY.

People don't tell me no, and when I call in favors to pull this off, everyone steps in to offer a hand.

Now here we are, standing in my living room, and I'm looking into Haven's eyes.

She's nervous, that much is true, but she's brave, and she's standing here with her hands in mine, looking into my eyes.

My brothers are not here, but they'll understand.

Chrissy is here because there's no way she was going to miss it.

The pastor is talking about in sickness and in

health, rich and poor, and when it's my turn to say I do, I say it without any hesitation.

To my surprise, so does Haven.

The room is so quiet, and I feel guilty. I know she said she wanted a small wedding, but now that we're in the thick of it, I feel guilty. She deserves a big wedding. She deserves people to ooh and aah over her beauty, and more than anything, I want everyone to know that she's taken and she's mine.

It's only after the preacher that we dragged out of bed pronounces us husband and wife that shock seems to take over.

I walk the preacher to the front door, leaving Chrissy and Haven together. After paying him, I walk back in and over to Haven. Chrissy hugs me and tells Haven congratulations. "Drive safe."

She rolls her eyes. "I live two doors down. I'll drive safe."

As soon as she's gone, I grab Haven's hand and pull her to the couch to sit down. "Where would you like to go for our honeymoon?"

She swallows. "Uh, I can't take off. I have a photoshoot next week. Plus, this is fake, King. We don't have to do the whole honeymoon thing."

"Don't say that," I demand.

"Don't say what? That this is fake? I know what

this is, and I think it's best that we both remember it."

I should be happy with what she's saying, but I'm not. I know what we talked about, and I know that I'm not capable of a real marriage with love and all that shit. This is the plan, and we should stick with it… so why do I want more? Why is it physically painful to me when she says this is fake? "The only people that know this isn't real is me and you."

She crosses her arms over her chest and juts her chin at me. "So your brothers and your sister think this is real?"

"I never said fake to them."

She tilts her head to the side like she's trying to understand. "Well, what exactly did you tell them?"

"I told them we planned to have a baby together."

She looks over my shoulder, and when I follow her gaze, I see that she's looking at the big framed picture of me, my brothers, and my sister. She gets up and walks across the room to take a closer look. "What did they say? Did they try and talk you out of it?"

I had told her I wouldn't lie to her anymore, and I plan to keep that promise. "Not really. They didn't understand because they know I'm not capable of love."

She hugs herself, and I wish I could see her face. She doesn't say anything. I stand up from the couch and walk over to her. As I get close, I stand behind her and wait for her to turn around. I'm sure she's overwhelmed right now, and I already pressured her into marrying me. I need to give her space.

When she doesn't turn around, I need to know she's all right. "Are you okay?"

She nods and finally turns to look at me. "I know I agreed to this, and I know what the goal is here… but I need time."

I hold my hands up. "There's no pressure, peaches. You have my ring on your finger. The rest can wait until you're ready."

The relief on her face says it all. I've taken full advantage of her, and I need to back off. I physically take a step back. "Callan should be here with your clothes soon. I put some of my sweats and T-shirts in your room if you want to sleep in them."

"My room?"

I nod and try to hide the dissatisfaction on my face. I want her in my bed. If it was up to me, that's exactly where she would be. But it's not up to me, and I'm already pushing my luck with her. The last thing I want is to spook her and have her run away from me. "Yeah, no pressure, Haven. We'll take it slow."

I can't tell if she's happy about it or not, but she points down the hall. "Which is my room?"

Fuck. I didn't even think about showing her around. Everything has been so rushed. "Come on, I'll give you the grand tour."

We start downstairs, and I take her through the living room, the kitchen, office, and spare guestroom. As we walk upstairs, I just point at my room, not wanting to stress her out, and then take her to the bedroom next to mine. "This is you. Or if you want another room, you can have it."

She looks around the room, and I'm fast to tell her, "You can make any changes you want." She keeps looking. "To any room in the house. I want you comfortable here, so you can redecorate or anything you want to do. This is your house, and you can do anything you want to it."

I go over to the curtains and draw them back. The backyard is dark, but the moonlight makes the pool shimmer. "There's a pool and a gym out back."

She sighs, and I can't help it, I have to look her

in the face. Standing next to her, I tell her, "Look at me, Haven."

She turns to look at me, and she looks lost. "Are you overwhelmed?"

When she doesn't answer, I reach for her, putting my hands on her shoulders. She doesn't flinch, but she doesn't open to me like she has been. "Tell me, baby, are you okay?"

She shudders a breath. "Honestly, I don't know."

I hold my arms out and wait to see what she wants. I'd give anything to hold her but only if she wants to.

It's only when she steps toward me and wraps her arms around my waist that I close my arms around her and hold her flush to my body. I know I fucked up, and that's all I seem to do with her. The need to claim her as mine overshadowed what she wanted. "Do you regret it?"

I hold my breath, waiting for her to answer. What will I do if she says yes? The right thing to do is give her an annulment, but I know I won't be able to do that. I can't let her go. If she'll give me time, I'll show her how good we could be together.

"No," she whispers against my throat.

My chest shudders, and I kiss the top of her

head. "Okay… me either. I'm sorry I rushed you, but I'm not sorry that you're mine." I lean back and lift her chin so I can look her in the eye. "Take all the time you need."

She nods, and I'm about to kiss her, but she buries her head against my chest. I hold on to her, knowing that I'm going to do everything I can to make sure she's happy.

19

HAVEN

"HAVE A SEAT. I'm putting breakfast on the table. Want coffee, orange juice, or water?"

I walked into the kitchen after smelling coffee but wasn't prepared to see King, shirtless, standing at the stove with a spatula in his hand and a smile on his face. I tug at the T-shirt I'm still wearing. The sweats were too hot to wear while sleeping, and I took them off, but now I'm kicking myself because I probably should have put them on before coming downstairs.

"Coffee, definitely coffee. But I can get it."

He waves the spatula. "Sit… I'll get it."

I look down and tug at the hem of my shirt. "I should probably go put pants on. I'll be right—"

Before I can finish, he says my name. "Haven."

I look up at him, but he's staring at my bare legs. "Stay," he commands.

"But—"

I stop as he pours coffee into a mug. "Cream or sugar?"

"Black."

He comes toward me and holds the cup out. "Stay. I've thought about your legs all night anyway. No need to cover them up."

I take the mug from him and try to avoid staring at his bare chest. "Thank you."

I walk toward the table and sit down, trying to get myself together. I barely slept last night. I know King was worried that I regretted getting married, but I don't. I think I was shocked by how sudden it all was, but honestly, I'm glad to have it over with. I was never the person that dreamed of a big wedding or anything. Hell, I never even imagined my wedding because I never dreamed I'd be getting married. I always thought that was a faraway thing that would never happen for me. Plus, it's not like I have any family that would come anyway. But now that I am married, I'm starting to dream about the future and what that could look like. I'm both excited and a little nervous.

"I wasn't sure what you'd like, so I fixed eggs,

bacon, toast, and oatmeal. I could make some French toast if you prefer."

I look around at the platters of food. I usually eat yogurt or something light for breakfast, but this is exactly what I need this morning. I was too nervous last night to eat anything. "This is perfect. So you cook? I'm impressed."

"Yeah, I enjoy it. Dig in."

He sits down next to me, and we both fill our plates. We eat in silence for a few minutes, and then he asks, "Did you sleep well?"

For the first time since we sat down, I really look at him and notice the redness of his eyes. He looks tired, and I wonder how he slept. "I didn't really sleep much. I feel like I tossed and turned most of the night."

He grips his fork a little tighter. "Was the bed uncomfortable? Or were you just worried about… things?"

"The bed was fine." Instead of answering his other question, I ask him, "What about you? Did you sleep okay?"

He groans and runs his hand through his beard. "I didn't sleep well at all. I was worried about you."

The sincerity on his face has me reaching for him. I touch his hand, and instantly he turns it and wraps his fingers around mine. "I'm fine. I don't regret last night. If anything, I'm glad it happened the way it did. I wouldn't want a big wedding with everyone looking and talking about me. I'm ready to move on and get on with our lives. I didn't sleep well because I felt bad… it was your wedding night—"

He interrupts me. "Our wedding night."

"Right. Our wedding night, and well, I'm sure you expected things to be different than sleeping in separate beds and—"

He cuts me off, leaning toward me. "Nope, I'm not expecting anything. You have my ring on your finger. The rest will fall into place. I told you I'm a patient man."

Damn, he's so handsome, and he knows all the right things to say to calm me and make it all right. "Okay."

He nods. "Okay." And then we continue to eat while he holds my hand.

It should feel weird or out of the ordinary, but it doesn't. All I can think is how it calms me that he's touching me the way he is.

"When's your next photo shoot?"

"The end of next week. My agent is working out the details. She wasn't happy with the photographer they had lined up, so I'm not sure if it's going to happen or not."

"Why not?"

I take a sip of my coffee and then scrunch my nose up. Just thinking of Axle puts a bad taste in my mouth. "The photographer is known for being handsy and inappropriate. My agent knows I don't do well with that."

"Who is it?"

"My agent?"

"No, the photographer."

He's stopped eating and has turned to me fully. I set my mug down and give him my full attention. "Why?"

His jaw tightens. "Because I wanna know. What's his name?"

My eyebrows raise. "I'm not telling you."

"Haven Beckett," he says, and I both get a thrill and am surprised. It's the first time I've heard my name said with my new last name.

I shake my finger at him. "Oh no, you think you're going to win me over by calling me that, but I'm still not telling you."

He shrugs. "I'll handle it."

My mouth falls open. "You'll handle it? You absolutely will not. No way."

"You're my wife, Haven."

I lift my hand up and hold it out to him. The rings he put on my finger last night are huge, and anyone within fifty feet would notice them. "Trust me, I know I am. This rock you gave me is hard to miss."

"You don't like it?" he says worriedly.

"I love it. It's big, and you spent too much money, but I love it. That's not the point. I know I'm your wife, but that doesn't mean you're going to 'handle things.' I can take care of it."

He lets go of my hand, and before I can miss his touch, he grabs the seat of the chair I'm sitting in and pulls me so that I'm right next to him. I suck in a breath at the closeness, but it's not because of panic or not wanting to be touched; it's because I'm anticipating it. He leans toward me until our lips are mere inches apart. "No man is going to get handsy with you, Haven. You're my wife. Mine."

I reach up and cup his jaw in my hand. It softens under my touch, but I can still see the determination on his face. "I know you want to throw your name around and take care of this for me, but I need you to let it go. If he stays on as the photographer, I can cancel the job. It's in my contract."

He wants to argue with me, but he surprises me with his request. "You're not going to quit a job because some man doesn't know boundaries. If he's the photographer, you let me go with you."

"Go with me?" I ask, shocked.

"Yes."

The fact that he wants to do this for me sends me into a tailspin. I keep reminding myself why we're doing this, and it's supposed to be fake, but why is it all starting to feel real?

"Okay. If he's the photographer, you can go with me."

He exhales and he's obviously relieved. "Okay." He points at my plate. "Eat."

I turn to the table and pick up my fork again, but not without murmuring, "You sure are bossy."

He just laughs.

When we finish eating and we're cleaning up, King stands next to me, taking the plate I just washed so he can dry it. "So I've got something to ask you."

I should probably be nervous because I'm finding he doesn't ask easy questions. "What?"

"If you have time, I have a project I'm working on. I had hoped it would be further along, and I could use your help with it."

He owns the biggest construction company in the South, and I know nothing about construction. "I'm not sure what I could do to help you, but I could give it a shot."

He laughs. "No, it's not help with the construction company. It's something else. I bought the building in front of the junior high school here in Whiskey Run."

He has my attention now. "I heard. Are you really putting in a community center?"

"Yeah, I want a safe place for kids to go to, and it's a perfect location. It's been gutted out and the interior is done, but it needs to be furnished and planned for day to day. I need to hire people, put together some kind of work schedule, an activity schedule and a thousand other things that I don't have time for. I need someone to oversee it." He raises his hands up. "Now I'm not trying to interfere with your job. I know it's important to you. I'm just wondering if you'd be interested in overseeing it. You can hire help. Eventually down the road, I want there to be classes for teaching them things about nutrition, online safety… I mean, I have all kinds of ideas, but I haven't been able to dedicate as much time to it as I need to."

I point at my chest. "And you want me to help?"

He nods, and I hop excitedly. "I would love to help, King. Can we go there today and look at it?"

Again, as soon as I agree, he seems to relax. It's almost like he was worried about asking me. He has no idea how important something like this is to me. I wish it had been around when I was growing up. Every kid needs a place to feel safe and go when their home lives are not what they should be. I put my hand to my chest, right over my heart, and repeat the words even though I know they're not enough. "I would love to be a part of this. Thanks for asking me to."

20

KING

IT'S LATE. I should be in bed, but I don't want to be because after spending the day with Haven, I don't want the night to end.

She's talked nonstop since we got home. Asking her to be a part of the community center project was a great idea. She has her notebook out and is writing down all the things she wants to do there. I was already excited about this project, but the way she's been giddy about it, it takes the excitement to a whole new level.

She sits down on the couch next to me, her hip next to mine, and I don't want to make any sudden movements because I don't want her to move. She's talking animatedly, and I can't take my eyes off her. I don't know if she realizes it or not, but she's touched my hand and reached for me more today than she ever has. I'm trying not to pressure her, but the more time I spend with her, the more I want her.

She stops mid-sentence and puts her hand on my forearm. "Thanks again for letting me help."

"Help? I think we talked about this earlier, didn't we? You're in charge, Haven. You get the final decision on things. You get a salary. You can hire an assistant to take over when you do your modeling or if you need time off. Whatever you want."

"You're not paying me, King."

"It's a job. You're not doing it for free. It's going to take a lot of your time."

She shakes her head side to side. "No, it doesn't feel right."

Somehow I need to make her understand. "I didn't marry you to get free labor, Haven. I don't expect you to do this out of the kindness of your big heart. It's going to take time out of your schedule. I'm paying you."

She squeezes my arm. "But do you have any idea what this place means to me already? This is amazing, King. For the first time in a long time, I feel like I'm doing something with purpose. I'm excited about something."

I sigh because I know exactly how she feels. I put up some of the biggest buildings in the city, but this thirty thousand square foot building means more to me than anything I've ever done.

She changes the subject and leans the side of her face against the couch as she looks at me. "Why a community center? You could put in a dozen other things that would make you money—why the community center?"

I shrug. "Why did you become a model?"

She's fast in her response. "The free clothes."

I don't believe her. There has to be more to it than that. "Now tell me the real reason."

She leans back. "I don't know. I spent most my life not being seen. My mom and dad didn't see me. I had to take care of myself; I had no one. For the first time, people were looking at me." She rolls her eyes. "Gah, that sounds so stupid, doesn't it?"

It pains me to know that she felt that way. I saw her across a parking lot and knew she was special. How could her mom and dad and everyone else that let her down not see her and not love her the way she should be loved? My voice is thick with emotion. "No, it's not stupid at all."

She nods her head. "Okay, your turn. Why a community center? I mean, you own the biggest construction company around here. You have thousands of employees. You have people lined up to get on your schedule and could stay busy for years and years... but you decided to do a community center. Why?"

I try not to think about the past a lot. I thought I'd moved on from the little boy that was scared all the time, but no matter how hard I tried to run away from my past, it always caught up to me. I'm figuring that this is the best way to heal my past and to help other kids that were just like me. "I told you that I was raised in foster homes."

She nods and looks at me expectantly, knowing there's more.

"Well, it was hard. It was hard for me. It was hard for Holden, Ledger, Dom, Gabe, and Chrissy. And a hundred other kids in this town. We needed help, and it felt like no one cared. I know that's crazy now, and there's a thousand people that would want to help these kids, but when you're living it, you feel like there's no one. I want to provide a place that helps kids. Kids like me but also kids like you and anyone else that needs it. I don't expect to change the world, but maybe if I can help some kids know that there are people willing to stand up for them and protect them, then I can change their world."

She leans her head against my chest and wraps her arm around my waist. She squeezes on to me, and I cover her hand with my own. The sensation of her against me feels right. I wish I could tell her how I feel about her, but I bite my tongue. She's not ready to hear it, and it's not like I can change the rules already. We've only been married a little over twenty-four hours.

A few moments pass by, and she whispers to me, "You're a good man, King."

I suck in a deep breath because her words hit me right in the chest. It means so much to me that she says that. If anything, she makes me want to be a better man. I hold her tighter, and even though I can't say it out loud, I say it in my head. *I want more with you, Haven. I know I said I wanted to do this because of my fuckin' reputation and I wanted to have kids, but the truth is, I can't let you go. I don't want to let you go. I wish I could say it to you and tell you how I feel, but I'm afraid that all I'll end up doing is pushing you away.*

Haven burrows herself into my side. "I should get up and go to bed."

"Or we could just stay here."

She raises up so she can see my face. "You have to be tired. Neither one of us slept last night."

I loosen my hold on her, but I don't let her go. I want her to make the decision. "I'm comfortable right here, but it's your choice, peaches."

I wish I could take her to our room and sleep in our bed, but I don't have that option. Not yet. I can see her debating, and I murmur, "Stay."

She settles against me. "If you want to give up your comfortable bed for this couch, who am I to argue with you?"

I bury my nose in her hair. "I'm choosing you over our bed, Haven."

Her fingers are tracing patterns on my chest, and it's driving me crazy, but I'm not going to stop her. Hell, it's like torture, but this is what I want. I want her to feel comfortable to touch me any way she wants.

Her hand continues exploring, and she has no idea how it affects me. "Okay, then. I choose you over my bed too."

I prop my feet up on the coffee table, put an arm around her shoulder, and pull her into me. "Is this okay?"

She snuggles into me. "It's perfect, King."

21

HAVEN

I STRETCH MY BODY, and the groan underneath me has me stopping suddenly. I freeze and try to replay everything about last night. The last thing I remember is lying on the couch with King.

He has one arm under me, one over me, and the same for his legs. It's like he's completely wrapped around me. I start to move, and he grunts, "Stay."

I let my head fall back to his chest. "You can't be comfortable."

He chuckles. "I dunno. I feel pretty good right now."

I stay frozen, half of my body on top of him. His hand presses into my back, holding me in place. My shirt must have raised up in the night because his hand is against my bare skin. "Are you okay? I mean, if you want to move, you can, peaches."

He's obviously worried about me and my intimacy issues, but it's funny because being in his arms feels good. I'm not thinking about trying to escape or wanting to push him away. If anything, I want more.

"I'm fine. I'm okay."

His fingers start to caress my back, and I tremble under his touch. "Good morning, wife."

I couldn't stop the smile if I wanted to. My body reacts in every way, and I shift a little on top of him.

He groans again, and that's when I feel it. His manhood is pressed against my hip. Heat rushes to my face. "Uh, how about you? You okay?"

His voice is gruff. Either from just waking up or because it's thick with emotion, I'm not sure. "I'm not going to act like I'm not attracted to you. Hell, I'm half hard all the time just looking at you, but I don't want to freak you out."

I shake my head, still unable to look at him. "You're not freaking me out." I trace a heart on his chest, and when I realize it's a heart, I start to trace other patterns. "Good morning, husband."

"You know what this means, don't you?"

"What what means?"

He presses his whole hand to the middle of my back, fitting my lower body flush to his. "You have to start sleeping in our bed from now on. Now that I know what it's like to sleep with my wife, I'm going to have to have you in my arms from now on."

Speechless, all I can do is nod. I have a thousand questions I want to ask him, but it's all becoming a blur. My silence has him trying to reassure me. "Don't panic, Haven. I have no expectations, and it's completely up to you. We can just sleep. No pressure."

I hope I don't regret this. "I'd like that."

He takes a deep breath and then lets it out. "All right, let's get going. We have a lot to do today."

Finally, I raise my head. "I thought you'd have to go into work today."

"I know you didn't want to go on a honeymoon, but I was hoping we could spend some time together. You think I can hang with you at the community center today?"

Excitement fills my voice. "You want to go with me?"

He smiles ear to ear. "I'd love to spend the day with you."

I climb off the couch, tugging at my clothes as I go. "I'll go get ready."

From where I'm standing, his hard manhood is evident, and after I look at the bulge between his legs, I force my eyes off him and hustle from the room.

After showering and getting ready, I meet King in the living room.

His gaze travels down my body and back up again. I chose jeans and a tank top to wear today because I wanted to be comfortable, but King seems to like my choice too. "You look beautiful, wife."

I giggle. "Are you going to call me that all day? Some people may be surprised that you're now married."

"It's fine. I'm not going to try and hide it. I talked to my brothers. Well, everyone except for Ledger. He's in the Middle East somewhere. But yeah, they all said congratulations and they can't wait to meet you."

I hold my breath. "Were they mad they weren't invited?"

"Please, none of my brothers would have wanted to get all dressed up anyway. And they understand why it was rushed."

He puts his hands in the front pocket of his jeans and plants his feet shoulder-width apart. The white T-shirt he has on is tight across his chest, and I catch myself staring at him. I smack my lips closed and shake my head. My husband is hot, capital H-HOT.

"You ready?"

I nod and follow him out the door. The community center is on the other side of town, but it doesn't take any time to get there. As soon as we're there, we get to work. There are people scheduled to come for interviews. A few painting companies are coming to put their bids in because the whole interior needs to be painted, and while we wait, I walk room to room with King, telling him my ideas. We go over everything, and it makes me feel good that King seems to like my plans.

"You can tell me no. You know that, right?"

He shrugs, his eyes set on my face even though I've caught him staring at my ass more times than not. "Yeah, I know, but why would I? You have some great ideas."

I look at him doubtfully, but before I can say anything, the front door opens. I look at my watch. "That's probably the painters."

King and I make our way to the front of the

building, and sure enough, there's a man waiting for us. "Hi. I'm Pete with Quality Painters." The man lets his gaze travel down my body and then back up again. I clasp my hands together in front of me. King comes to stand beside me, and by the tense look on his face, it's obvious he saw the man looking at me too. "Hello. I'm Haven and this is my husband, Ridge." I turn to King. "Honey, would you care to show Pete around and tell him what we're wanting to do?"

"I'd be happy to."

I'm standing over my notebook as the two men disappear to the back of the building. It isn't long before they come to the front and Pete is leaving, telling us he'll get the bid in soon.

As soon as Pete walks out the door, King crowds me. "I'm going to have to hire a bodyguard."

His nostrils are flared as he stares down at me. "A bodyguard?" I ask, incredulous.

He grabs my hand and holds it, rubbing his fingers over the ring. "Fuck, I thought the ring was big enough, but some guys don't care. I don't like the way he looked at you. How am I supposed to leave you here when there are men like that wanting what's mine?"

Maybe I shouldn't enjoy it as much as I am, but

it feels good to have a man want me the way King does. He doesn't try to hide it or his attraction to me. He acts as if he's proud that I'm his wife and wants everyone to know it. King doesn't have to worry about me with other men because no one compares to him. "I don't want them."

He growls with possession in his eyes. "Tell me you're mine, peaches."

I laugh. "I don't know what else I gotta do, King. I married you. I have your ring on my finger. I woke up in your arms… I'm yours."

He gruffs, "Yes, you are."

We stand here staring at each other, neither one of us moving. He's staring at my lips, and finally I ask him, "What are you looking at?"

"Your pretty mouth."

I stutter, "My mouth?"

He leans down and repeats it. "Your pretty mouth."

He lifts his hand and traces his finger around my lips. It's so sensual that my nipples pebble and there's a pull in my lower belly.

I'm breathless as I ask him, "Are you going to kiss me… or what?"

His hands come to my waist, and he pulls me flush to his body. My heart starts to race, and I take a deep breath to try and calm myself. He cups my face in his hands and leans down, pressing his lips to mine.

He takes complete possession of my mouth and is relentless as he kisses me until I've leaned into him and let him consume me. The kiss is intense, and I meet him stroke for stroke with my tongue. Heat envelops me as he circles his arms around my body and cradles me against him.

I slide my hands to his waist, lifting his shirt and putting my hands against his bare skin. He sucks in a breath and pulls away with a groan when he rests his forehead against mine. I'm doing my best to catch my breath, and when I open my eyes, he pulls back. "You're an obsession, peaches."

I swallow hard because I could say the same thing about him.

22

———

KING

I LIE AS STILL as I can, but it's nearly impossible. Haven slept in our bed last night, and even though we started out on opposite sides of the bed, she's now on top of me.

She's still asleep, but she has my leg fitted between hers, and she's sliding her panty-covered pussy against my leg. I bite my lip to stifle the groan, but I'm not going to be able to hold back much longer. My cock is hard, seeping precum, and with each slide of her pussy against me, I get harder.

She whimpers in her sleep, and I know exactly what she needs.

I put my hands on her, and even though I hate to do it, I know I need to. "Haven."

She rubs against me again. Fuck me, I'm not going to survive this.

"Haven, baby, wake up."

I know the instant she becomes alert because her whole body tautens on top of me. She knows what she's been doing without me having to tell her. She moans and leans her face against my bare chest. "Oh my God, kill me now."

I'm taking deep breaths, trying to control my breathing because I'm seconds from coming in my shorts. "It's okay."

She groans and shakes her head. "Oh my God, it's not okay. I'm humping your leg in my sleep, King. It's definitely not okay."

She tries to jerk away from me, but I hold on to her, refusing to let her go. I feel that we've come so far, and there's no way I'm letting this set us back. "Stop, you're not going anywhere."

She stops struggling, but she won't look at me. "This is so embarrassing, please just let me get up."

This is going to be torture for me, but I don't care. I need to turn this situation around before she tries to hide from me the rest of the day. "There's no reason to be embarrassed."

"Arrgh." She groans again.

I use my body to force her on her back and

hover over her. Her eyes are wide as she stares up at me. I have my hands on hers, and I'm holding them to the mattress over her head. "Don't be embarrassed."

She clenches her eyes shut. "I was having a dream and…" She stops talking and shakes her head side to side.

I lean down and whisper to her, "And what… you were having a dream and what, peaches?"

"I was dreaming we were… you know."

I raise my knee up the bed, right to her core, and her hips flex under me. She's practically vibrating.

"You need to come, don't you?"

Her eyes fly open, and I reassure her, "No pressure… but I could make you come, Haven. Let me take care of you."

"But—"

I interrupt her. "No sex, not until you're ready. I'll use my mouth and my hands, that's it."

She lifts her head as I keep rotating my knee along her swollen clit. "Your mouth?"

I nod, and I'm practically salivating to get a taste of her.

When she doesn't answer, I try not to plead, but even I can hear it in my voice. "You can tell me no.

I'll let you up, and you can forget this ever happened. Or you can let me do this… let me taste you."

I'm cheating because I nudge my leg along her swollen core, and she tosses her head back. "I need—"

She stops talking, and I lean down. "Tell me, Haven. Tell me what you need… what you want."

"I need to come," she confesses with her eyes shut.

"Look at me. I need you to look at me and say it."

She opens her eyes and stares up at me. I search for any type of hesitancy or denial, but all I see is desire. She's eaten up with it. "I need to come, husband."

Now it's my turn. The guttural groan comes from deep in my chest, and my cock gets harder. Her calling me husband is my undoing.

I inhale deeply and let it out slowly, hoping to gain some control of my body's reaction to her. This is all about her.

While looking into her eyes, I trail my hand down her body. I slide my fingers under the waistband of her underwear, and she sucks in a breath.

"It's okay," I tell her.

I kiss her lips before kissing down her body. I would give anything to strip her clothes off her, but that wasn't part of the deal. I push her thighs open and settle myself between them. Sitting on my haunches, I stare down at her panty-clad pussy. The way she's been gyrating on my leg has her panties pulled tight with a wet spot along her slit.

I grab on to the side of her panties and pull the material, ripping along the seams. Her body jerks, and she raises up on her elbows to glower at me. "Was that necessary?"

"I'll buy you new ones."

I do the same on the other side and then pull the material away from her body. The scent of her arousal fills my nose, and I breathe out slowly. *Keep it together, Beckett.*

I press my fingers to her core, spreading her open and sliding along her swollen slit. Her hips raise up to meet my touch, and I smile, feeling the control I have over her body. "You're so wet for me."

Her legs open farther, and I show her my approval by circling her clit with my finger. "I need to taste you, Haven."

I give her a chance to deny me, but she looks

right into my eyes and nods her head. I don't hesitate and lean in to taste her. In one smooth motion, I lick her from hole to clit. She whimpers, and her hands go to my shoulders, her nails digging into my skin as I suck her clit between my lips.

"Oh wow…oh, please don't stop," she begs, and I smile as I increase the pressure on her swollen nub.

Her hips are thrusting against me, and I devour her. I slide a finger inside her, and she's so fuckin' tight I can't help but wonder how I'm ever going to fit inside. I pump into her, small gentle strokes of my finger, and she comes undone. Her body flexes as the orgasm takes over her body. I lick her release and can't get enough of her.

Only when she's limp on the bed, panting, do I stop.

I crawl up her body and lean over her, searching her dazed eyes. "Are you okay?"

She nods her head. "That was… wow."

I press my lips to hers, and she smiles against my mouth. Her hand comes up, and she strokes my beard with her fingers. "You have me on you."

I lean over her, trying to keep my weight off her. My cock is still hard, and I know I'm going to need to take care of it in the shower. "I like having you on me." I roll to my side. "I need to get up. I have a meeting this morning in Jasper."

She sits up and watches me as I sit down on the edge of the bed. I try to hide the pain of my hard-on. I don't want her to feel bad or lacking in any way. I definitely don't want her to think she needs to sleep in the other room because I can't control myself.

She stretches behind me and moans, sounding satisfied. "I'm going to go to the community center today."

I take a deep breath. "Call if you need me, okay?"

She says okay, and I get up, keeping my back to her. I know my underwear are stuck to me because they're soaked with precum. I walk into the bathroom and take a quick shower. I only have to fist myself and stroke it three times and I'm coming on the shower floor.

I try to be quiet, but the release is amazing, and I'm moaning Haven's name as the orgasm rolls through my body.

I take a quick shower, hating that I'm washing her scent off me, and when I come into the bedroom with my towel around my waist, she's nowhere to be found. I throw some clothes on and check the spare bedroom before descending the stairs. She's in the kitchen and she looks at me smugly as she hands me a to-go mug of coffee.

"Thank you."

She nods. "Of course. I, uh, heard you in the shower. I'm sorry… I wasn't even thinking… That had to be painful for you."

I put my hand on her chin and pull it up so she's looking at me. "Seeing you come undone was everything to me. I told you no pressure, and there's no pressure. I'm happy you let me taste you."

"But—" she starts, and I interrupt her.

"No buts. That was perfect, Haven, and I wouldn't change a thing."

She finally nods her head and leans up on her tiptoes to kiss me. The fact she's the one initiating the kiss makes it even better. I want her to trust me. I pat her ass. "Remember who you belong to, Mrs. Beckett."

She doesn't hesitate. "You."

I hold her to me and kiss her until we're both breathless. "See you later, wife."

"Bye, husband."

I almost got out of here and forgot to tell her, "Hey, I'm driving myself today. Callan is waiting outside to take you wherever you need to go."

She is coming toward me. "I'm not taking your driver, King. That's ridiculous. I'm in Whiskey Run."

I lean down and kiss her. "This is a non-negotiable, Haven. I can't work if I don't know you're safe."

"But—"

I kiss her again. "Please, do this for me."

She juts her chin at me. "How am I supposed to say no to that?"

"You're not."

She lets out a huff. "Fine. We'll do it your way, Mr. Beckett."

With one last kiss, I reluctantly walk out the door, and as soon as I get into my car, I let out a big breath. I would give anything to stay here all day, but unfortunately I have meetings today that could cost me fourteen million dollars if I blow them off.

I barely get on the road and my phone is ringing. Seeing my human resource manager's name on the caller ID, I hit the button on my dashboard to answer it. "Ridge."

Becca starts talking, and it's so fast, I can't make out a word. "Becca, slow down. I can't understand you."

She breathes in. "Is it true? Did you get married?"

I had let my assistant know I got married and would be out of the office a few days. I'm not used to answering to anyone, so I'm not sure what this is about. "Yes, it's true."

"To who?" Becca asks.

I'm proud of having Haven as my wife, and I don't even hesitate in naming her. "I married Haven Weston… well, now she's Mrs. Haven Beckett. Is there a reason you're asking? I can add her to my insurance today. I'll send over all the information to you."

"I didn't even know you were dating someone."

I take my eyes off the road in front of me and look at the screen of my phone that is displayed on the dashboard. "Becca, I'm not sure what you're asking me, but my personal life is really none of your business and—"

She cuts me off. "I know, sir, but I was here when your mom showed up after you made the Forbes list. She wanted your money, and I just think it's weird that all of a sudden, out of the blue, some woman—"

I don't let her finish. "Becca, don't finish that statement. Haven is my wife, and I will not have her talked about in this manner. You are in charge of human resources for Beckett Construction, and that's your only concern."

She's quiet on the other end, and I almost wonder if she's hung up. "Do we understand each other, Becca?"

She still quiet, and when she finally answers, she sounds angry. "Yes, sir."

I press the button to end the phone call and step on the gas. Anger fills me. I hate even thinking of my mother. She gave me up when I was little. She lived in Whiskey Run the whole time and never came to get me, never saw me or anything. It wasn't until I made that list that she came to see me, wanting money. How dare Becca compare Haven to my mother? Haven is nothing like her.

I am fuming mad the rest of the way to my offices in Jasper. I would give anything to go back and spend the rest of the day with Haven, but I can't. I need to do this meeting, and then I need to get my office in check. They will respect my wife… or they'll lose their jobs.

23
____

HAVEN

I STARE INTO THE DARKNESS, on my side of
the bed, and wish I could at least see King's face.
We've been lying here for an hour now, and neither
one of us can seem to fall asleep. All I'm thinking
about is what he did to me this morning, and I want
more of that, but I'm too shy to ask him for it.

"I have a favor to ask."

He rolls toward me, and even though I can feel
his eyes on me, I can't see him. I sit up in the bed
and turn the bedside lamp on.

We both squint at the sudden light, but he
doesn't complain. He sits up in the bed next to me.
"Anything."

I look over at him, see his bare chest, and try to

concentrate on what I was saying. "You can tell me no."

He leans up on one elbow and smiles at me. "I think you know I'm not going to tell you no."

"But you don't know what it is."

He shrugs. "Fine. Tell me what it is."

I bite my lip because I've been nervous about this since I talked to Cassie earlier today and she came up with the idea. I should have just told her no, but I felt so bad for not telling her about the wedding. "So you know my friend, Cassie?"

He thinks about it and then nods. "Yes. Best friend. Her husband is a police officer. Her brother-in-law is Walker."

"Right. Yeah, right that's her. Anyway, well, it's just that…"

He sits up in the bed, scooting up so his back is against the headboard. "Just tell me, peaches."

I blow out a breath. "Fine. I felt bad for not inviting her—heck I didn't even tell her about the wedding, and when she came to see me today, I felt so bad. She said we should do a party to sort of celebrate our marriage since no one got to celebrate the day with us. I know it's crazy-"

He cuts me off. "I think it's a great idea."

Shocked, I'm already thinking of all the reasons

it's a bad idea. "But I mean, that's crazy, right? I could probably just not say anything about it and hope she forgets it."

He pushes my hair off my shoulder and leans over so he can see my face. "Do you not want a party?"

I shrug. "I mean, it could be fun. I know I said I wanted a small wedding, but it feels weird. It's like we were trying to hide it or something. You know the town gossip is running wild, and everyone's trying to figure out how we got married and why it was all hush-hush."

"Who's talking? Tell me who it is and I'll set them straight. Fuck that, I'll put a full page ad—no, I'll buy every ad space in the paper and let them all know we got married."

I shake my head and laugh. "Stop. That's a little overboard, even for you. I'm just saying it would be nice to have a party, that's all."

He nods. "We'll do it then. Do you want to hire a party planner?"

"Cassie is on summer break, and she wants to plan it."

He nods. "I'll leave you my card in the morning. Spare no expense."

"But—"

He puts his hand on my shoulder. "Haven, honey, I have felt guilty on how I rushed you into the wedding. I want to do this, and I wish I'd thought of it. Let's do it right. Food, dancing, cake, decorations… all of it."

"But… are you sure?"

He cups my chin in his hand and searches my eyes. "I'm positive."

"Okay."

We look into each other's eyes, and just when I'm sure he's about to kiss me, he releases me, goes to his side of the bed, and lies down.

I reluctantly reach over and turn the light back off before lying down. I toss and turn a few minutes and sigh loudly in the room.

"Are you okay?"

I stare up at the ceiling. "Yeah."

The bed dips, and I know he's turning toward me, but he doesn't touch me, and I sigh again. Even though we can't see each other, I clench my eyes shut and ask him, "Have you changed your mind?"

"About the party?"

I'm messing this up so badly. "No, about me."

He almost sounds angry. "Why would you ask that?"

"I don't know. This morning we, ya know, and

then this evening you haven't touched me, and now even though you're right next to me, you might as well be a hundred miles away."

It's almost like I can hear his teeth grinding. "Because I don't trust myself, that's why."

I turn on the light again, and when I turn back to face him, he's lying on his back, eyes closed. "What do you mean you don't trust yourself?"

"Because I'm trying to be patient, Haven, but my body has a mind of its own. I tasted you this morning, and I'm doing my damndest to honor your wish of no pressure. Fuck, peaches, just lying in this bed next to you, my dick's so hard I could hammer nails."

He groans and rubs his hands across his face. I let my gaze travel down his body, and I stop at the tent of the sheets between his thighs. I lean up to get a closer look. "King."

"Yeah?" he mutters, half out of patience.

"Can I touch you?"

He sucks in a harsh breath and opens his eyes. He's hopeful but trying to hold back. "You don't have to."

I nod, moving my eyes down his body and resting on the juncture of his thighs. "Can I?"

Huskily, he says, "Peaches, you never have to ask to touch me."

I hook my finger into the sheet that's draped at his waist. Slowly, I pull it down his thighs and then off the bed to let it fall to the floor. He has on boxer shorts, but they're doing nothing to contain him. I look up at him, and he's staring at me. "Should I…?"

"Whatever you want, Haven. There's no wrong way… not with us."

I take a calming breath and then put my hands on each side of his waistband and pull the boxers down his hips. His manhood springs up when it's been uncovered, and I gasp at the sheer size of him. I finish removing his shorts, letting them fall to the floor with the sheet and then sit back on my haunches to stare at him. Just while I'm watching, I can see the bead of moisture at his tip form.

I crawl over his leg and position myself on the bed between his legs. I've never been so nervous and so excited about something in my life. He pushes my hair away from my face. "Look how hard you make me, peaches."

I let my hands trail up his thighs and then I tentatively wrap my hand around his girth. His hips flex, his head falls back, and he groans.

Afraid that I've hurt him, I loosen my hold on him, but he's shaking his head. "No, don't stop. It just feels good, that's all."

Surprise at the fact that I've pleased him just by touching him urges me on. I hold him firmer in my hands and then start to explore. I stroke him from root to tip. I smear the precum along his shaft and then I stroke him again.

"Can I taste you, King?"

He grips the bed sheets in his hands. "Fuck, baby, you keep talking like that and I'm going to come."

I shrug, not seeing the problem. "That's what you want, right? You want to come?"

He leans up on his elbows. "When I come, I want to come inside you."

My mouth forms a perfect "O," and he nods. "Yeah, so touch me all you want, but I'm not coming until I'm deep inside you."

"Okay." I nod.

I spread his precum along his shaft again and then lean over and kiss his tip. He inhales sharply, but I don't stop. I let him slide in my mouth, and I take him as far down my throat as I can and then off. Over and over, I taste him, swirling my tongue around him and then taking him down my throat.

His hips are pumping slightly, and the more comfortable I get, the deeper I take him and the more I let myself go.

I moan roughly, and before I know it, I'm flipped onto my back with a very out of control King hovering over me. He's panting, "Enough. I need inside you."

I'm not sure what he expected, but he seems surprised when I open my legs and let his body fit against mine. "Okay."

His body is flush against me. His cock is hard, nestled between my thighs, and I find that if I shimmy just right, it slides along my clit.

"Fuck me," he grunts.

I lift my hips against him. "I'm trying to, if you'd cooperate."

I'm reaching for him, and he grabs my hands and pushes them above my head, holding them there. He leans over me. "Are you sure about this?"

I lean up and peck him on the lips. "I've practically thrown myself at you, King. I'm not sure what else I can do to show you I want this and I'm ready."

He grabs the hem of my shirt and starts to pull it up my body. I sit up to help him take it off, and as soon as I lie back down, he's pulling at my underwear. I intervene before he rips another pair. As soon as they're off, I'm lying underneath him, putting my hands to his chest. "Do you want the lights off?"

His gaze travels down my body. "No, I want to see you."

24

KING

HER PUSSY IS puffy and glistening for me. I want to drive into her and scream "mine" at the top of my lungs, but I hold myself back.

She's lifting her hips, wanting her release, and I'm determined to make her first time good.

I lean up and look into her face. There's so much trust in her eyes as she lies staring up at me. "Kiss me," I demand.

She lifts her head, and I seal my lips to hers. There's no holding back anymore because knowing she's about to be mine is fueling me like never before. I absolutely ravage her lips, claiming them until they're swollen. I kiss down her neck, nipping at her sweet skin along the way. Cupping her breasts in my hands, I pluck her cherry nipples and roll them between my thumb and forefinger. She whimpers and moans, but I know she's liking it because her fingernails are digging into my back, holding me closer.

I suckle her breast and then lave the other one with attention. I move back and forth until she's begging me for more. I slide one hand between her thighs and find her soaked for me.

"Please," she begs.

"You need to come, peaches?"

"Yes." She whimpers.

I circle her clit with my finger, and she clenches around me. She's so ready, and I move into position, lifting her hips a little, and then wrapping my hand around my girth and sliding it along the outside of her pussy.

She wiggles her body, trying to get me where she wants me, and when my tip hits her clit, she comes undone. She's so fuckin' responsive that already her body is cresting and her pussy floods with her orgasm. I can't take my eyes off her as she comes. When her breathing starts to even out, I let my dick rest along the seam of her pussy. "You still going to let me in, peaches?"

Her hands go to my chest, and she traces her fingers along my skin. I'm sweating from holding back, but I've reached the point where I need to come.

Her legs open wider. "I'm ready."

I slide my cock along her slit, and her arousal coats me. I fist my cock and position it at her entrance. Slowly, I enter her, and she takes a deep breath. "You're doing so good. That's right, baby, take me. Take all of me."

Her eyes are now wide as saucers. I'm taking my time, moving a little, letting her adjust to the size of me before I sink into her a little deeper. She groans, and I give her some encouragement. "Almost, Haven. I'm almost there."

"Do it. Just do it."

I hate the idea of hurting her, but I do as she says and slam into her the rest of the way. She winces and lets out a loud grunt as her pussy clenches on to me. It's like having my cock in a vise she's so tight, but she feels so good.

I slowly withdraw and then slide back in. The friction is everything, and I'm completely consumed by her. I look at where we're connected and watch as I move in and out of her. She moans as the pain turns to pleasure. "Look at how good you're taking me, peaches."

"It feels so good, King. I had no idea..."

Her voice trails off, and I know she didn't plan to wait for me, but knowing I'm her first—her last—is everything to me. "Can you give me one more? I want to feel you come all around me, Haven."

I'm pushing in and out of her, and she's shaking her head. The feeling is so intense, she half-whispers, "I can't. I can't."

I reach between us and slide my finger around her swollen clit. Her body tenses, and she groans as I continue to stroke her insides.

"Give me one more, peaches. I need to come, but I want us to come together."

I apply more pressure to her clit and drive into her as the orgasm comes on all of a sudden. She bears down on me until I can barely move, but I don't stop until she's sucking me in and I'm painting her insides with my cum.

The orgasm takes over my whole body until I'm a trembling mess, but I give in to it, grunting Haven's name over and over.

When I can't take another thing, I hover over her, holding my weight on my arms. We're both breathless, and I stare at her as she tries to pull herself together. I swipe the hair off her face. "Are you okay?"

She smiles widely at me. "Okay? I'm more than

okay. I had no idea that could feel like that. I swear it felt like I was having an out-of-body experience at one point."

I lie down next to her and pull her into my arms. "It will be better next time."

She's in awe. "Better? I don't see how."

"It won't hurt next time."

She settles her head against my chest. "It only hurt for a minute, and then you made it feel good."

I kiss the top of her head. I didn't want to hurt her, so I'm glad I was able to make it good for her. "We need to clean up a little."

I don't want to get out of bed, but I know we have to. I stand up and then reach for her hand. She stands up to follow me and smiles. "So, uh, when can we do that again?"

As I turn on the water and wait for it to get hot, I have her held against me. "You're going to be sore after that, Haven. You may need a day or two to rest."

She gives me a sour look. "Oh, okay."

I pat her on the ass before squeezing it and pulling her under the spray of the water. "There's other things I can do, though… like this morning."

Her eyes light up. "This morning… yeah, that was good too."

I chuckle. "Well, I'm glad you approve because I'm going to need more of that. I thought about it all day."

She puts her arms around my neck. I don't discount what it means to have her reaching for me and holding her arms around me. I know this is something that she needs, but I didn't realize that I needed it just as much as she does. She plants a kiss on my chest. "I thought about it all day too."

I bury my face in her neck and inhale deeply. "I don't think I'll ever get enough of you, peaches."

I'm not sure, but I think I hear her murmur, "I hope not."

25

HAVEN

"YOU'RE GOING TO BE BORED."

"I'm not," he insists.

I roll my eyes. "This is not fun. It's a lot of standing around while they figure out lighting, space, direction. Well, in your case, it will be a lot of sitting around."

He stops, and since he's holding my hand, he pulls me to a stop with him. "Do you not want me to go in with you?"

We're standing outside of the studio where I'm supposed to do a photoshoot today. It's with Axle, the handsy photographer, and King has insisted on coming with me.

Of course I want him with me, but I feel bad. The man is being pulled in a thousand different directions, and he shouldn't have to come here and babysit me. "Of course I want you with me, but you were on the phone the whole way here. Whoever you were talking to was not happy about you missing a meeting today."

"It doesn't matter. None of that matters. I may have to work a little while I'm here——"

"I could have just canceled. Not now, because it's too late, but I could have last week."

He cups my face in his hands. "You will never quit a job because some man thinks it's okay to touch you."

I can't help but look at him worriedly, and he shakes his head. "You just go in there and do your thing. I'll take care of the rest."

I put my hands at his waist and tug at his shirt. Today he's in a jacket and tie, and he takes my breath at the way he fills his suit. "Are you going to be nice?"

He kisses the tip of my nose. "I'm always nice. Now let's go. You don't want to be late."

I get halfway through the door and stop. "Oh, I forgot to tell you. Today, I'm modeling pajamas."

His hand grips my waist. "Pajamas?"

I smile up at him. "Well, lingerie."

He lets his head fall down to his shoulders and grunt-whispers, "Well, fuck me."

I pat him on the shoulder. "We can do that after."

I walk away from him before I ask him to take me out of here and make good on his promise. It's been days since he's been inside me because he's worried that I'd be sore, and I'm over the waiting. I may have to take things into my own hands.

As soon as I get inside, I'm whisked away to hair and makeup and don't even get to introduce King to everyone. I gnaw on my lip as Katie does my hair, and when she gets to my makeup, she comments, "Whatever you're doing, keep it up. You're absolutely glowing."

I can feel the heat rise in my cheeks, but there's no way I can tell her than I'm glowing because I'm in love. As soon as I think it, I set back in my chair with a thud. I'm in love. I'm not supposed to be in love, that wasn't part of the plan, but I'd be a fool if I didn't guess this would happen.

I smile when my friend and fellow model Angel sits down in the chair next to me. "Hey, girl!"

"Hey, how you doing, Angel?"

She sits back while the hairdresser starts on her

hair. "I'm good. I saw your boyfriend having a talk with Axle."

I knew he'd say something. King is not the type to just sit back and wait for something to happen. "He's my husband."

Angel, the makeup artist, and the beautician all stop and stare at me. "You're married?" Angel asks.

I hold my hand up as if I need to show proof, but heck, sometimes I don't believe it myself. "Yep."

They all give me a round of congratulations, and I sit and listen to them talk about the last date Angel went on. After changing clothes, I look in the mirror. I know King is going to love seeing me in this outfit, but he's going to hate that other men will see me too.

As soon as we're ready, I walk back into the area for shooting, and King and Axle are still talking. When King sees me, his eyes travel down my body and then back up again. His jaw tightens, and he says something to Axle and then walks over to me. He has his arms open, and I step into them. He leans down, kisses my bare shoulder, and then whispers, "You look beautiful."

My heart stutters in my chest. I don't know if there's anyone better than this man. He makes me feel everything. "Thank you."

He pats me on the ass. "And when I get you out of here, I'm taking you home to bed and not letting you up until you have no doubt who you belong to."

I put one hand at his neck. "I know who I belong to."

He blows out a breath. "I hate that other men are going to see you like this."

I can relate to what he's saying. He's not up parading half naked in front of other women, but I do hate the way women always look at him. "I'm going home with you, though."

He grunts. "Hopefully, that will get me through the next few hours."

I watch him walk over to the corner and sit down. I expect him to pull out his phone, but he doesn't. Instead, he sits in his seat and watches me. The whole time, he never takes his eyes off me.

I can see him tense when Axle comes toward me, but Axle never gets within reach of me. If something needs adjusted, he has Katie do it. He is completely professional through the whole photo shoot. When it's over, I get dressed and then meet King by the door. As soon as I'm within arm's length of him, he's circling his arms around me and pulling me through the door.

We get outside, and Callan is standing at the

back of the car with the door already open. "Thanks, Callan. Take us to the penthouse. I need to show Haven our apartment here in the city."

"Yes, sir."

As soon as I get in the car, King is sliding in behind me. I knew he mentioned an apartment in Jasper, but that's all I'd heard about it. "The penthouse?"

He nods. "Yeah—" He gets cut off when his phone rings. He pulls it from his pocket and holds it up for me. "It's Chrissy."

"You need to answer it to make sure she's okay."

He seems to debate it for all of two seconds before answering. "Hey, sis, we're kind of busy."

26

KING

I LISTEN to my sister talk, and she's so excited I don't interrupt her. "I got Dom, Gabe, and Holden all together. Meet us for dinner."

"We're in Jasper, sis."

"Oh." She so disappointed I can hear it in her voice. "Okay, the boys were wanting to meet Haven, but sure, I understand. I can cancel dinner."

"Hold on." I take the phone from my ear. "Chrissy, Dom, Gabe, and Holden are wanting to meet for dinner."

She looks at me curiously. "Do you want me to meet your brothers?"

My forehead creases, and she lifts her shoulders in a shrug. "Well, I wasn't sure. They weren't at the wedding, and I mean, it's no big deal if you'd rather—"

I put the phone back to my ear. "Yeah, we'll be there. When and where?"

Chrissy cheers excitedly. "Yay! Okay, well, we're meeting at the Whiskey Whistler."

I groan. "That's a bar, sis. Not a place for dinner."

"What? It's fine. They serve food."

"Fine. We'll be there in thirty minutes. Bye, sis."

As soon as I hang up, I pull Haven onto my lap. She comes with a squeal, and she's shaking her head with laughter. "Uh, what's happening here?"

I hit the intercom. "Cal, change of plans. We're going to the Whiskey Whistler."

"Got it, sir."

With Haven on my lap, I use my legs to spread hers. The move makes her skirt raise up, and I help by pulling it up until she's fully exposed. "King, Callan will—"

I kiss the side of her neck. "Callan can't see anything through the partition. I planned to take you to the apartment and fuck you, but I'm going to have to settle on making you come and licking you off my fingers."

She whimpers as I slide my hand down the front of her underwear and pet her pussy. Her back arches, and she presses her ass against my hard cock. She's already wet for me, and I slide my digits through her swollen core. The ride to Whiskey Run is filled with me taking her to the edge and then letting off before she comes. She's so far gone by the time we cross the city limits that she's begging for me to let her orgasm.

"Please, King," she pleads with me.

I then circle her clit, and it's only a few strokes and her hips are thrusting, pressing into my hand, as she rides her orgasm.

When her moans become loud, I turn her head and seal my lips over hers. I swallow her moans, and when she comes off her high, I lift my hand up and suck her arousal off each of my fingers.

"Fuck, you taste good."

She slides off my lap and looks out the window. "Oh my God, we're here."

I laugh and straighten my tie and jacket. I know I'm rumpled, which is not usual for me, but there's nothing I can do about it now. I wouldn't change anything in the last thirty minutes. "You're beautiful."

I reach for her and adjust her dress for her. "Ready?"

She sucks in a breath and lets it out. "As ready as I'm going to be."

I get out of the car and then help her out. Callan steps out. "We're going to meet my brothers and sister to eat. Want to join us?"

He shakes his head. "I'm good. I'm going to walk around town a bit."

He walks down the sidewalk, and I grab Haven's hand to walk with her into The Whistler. As soon as we walk in, I hear someone bellow my name, and we walk over to the table where my brothers and sister are.

Chrissy is the first to wave at Haven, and she must have told our brothers about how Haven is not accustomed to hugs because instead of them picking her up in a bear hug, they each wave at her as I introduce them. "You know Chrissy. This is Dom, Gabe, and Holden. You'll get to meet Ledger next month."

Her cheeks are pink, and she nods her head and waves at each of them. "It's nice to meet you all."

We order food and drinks, and before I know it, Haven has each of my brothers wrapped around her finger. They're all laughing and joking around with each other, and I sit back in my chair and watch as my wife opens up and lets them in. I wasn't sure about it. I hoped she'd like them, but it seems like I was worried for nothing.

"All right, guys, I'm ordering food. I'm just going to order a bunch of appetizers since you all are more interested in drinking than anything else."

I lean down to whisper in Haven's ear, "You okay?"

She smiles wide at me. "Yes, I'm good."

Dom waves me off. "Go on, big brother. We'll take care of your wife while you're gone."

I point my finger at him. "Keep your hands off my wife, Dom, or I'll beat you like I did when we were teenagers."

He just laughs and chugs his beer.

I walk away without a worry. I know my brothers and have no doubt that Haven is safe with them. I walk up to the bar and order two of all the apps and another round of beers. I pull out my credit card as my brother Holden walks up beside me. "Want me to get this round?"

I hold up my card and hand it over to the server. "I got it. Good game last week."

He nods. "Thanks!" He takes a drink of his beer and gestures back to the table. "I get it now."

Confused, I shake my head. "Get what?"

"I didn't understand the other night when you were telling me about getting married. After finally meeting Haven and seeing you two together, I get it. She's good for you."

I catch Haven looking at me, and I wink at her. "Yeah, she is."

Holden leans against the bar. "So have you told her?"

The server comes and hands me my credit card, and then she shoves a piece of paper in front of Holden. "Can I have your autograph and can I get a picture with you?"

"Sure can," he says.

As the woman comes around the counter, one of her co-workers comes to take the picture. My brother hangs his arm around her shoulders, and they both smile for the camera. All I can do is shake my head. He's always had women falling at his feet, and I can't wait for the day he finds the one. Then he'll really understand it.

As soon as he's done with the picture, he comes back over to me and slaps me on the shoulder. "As I was saying, did you tell her that you love her?"

I'm about to deny it, but there's no use. I do love Haven, and somehow I need to convince her that I want this fake arrangement to be real. I shake my head. "I haven't told her yet, brother. But I plan to."

27

HAVEN

THE DAY HAS BEEN a busy one, but I'm still on a high from this morning with King. He wouldn't let me out of bed until he'd taken me twice, and even then he didn't seem to want to let me go.

I try to push everything, all my worries, to the back of my mind as I try to take care of everything at the community center. I'm checking off the list, and for everything I mark off, I add two more things that I just remembered that need to be done.

It's almost noon when the front door opens. "Chrissy, what are you doing here?"

She rolls her eyes, walking in with a big bag from what looks like Red's Diner. "My brother insisted I come to check on you, and so I thought I'd bring lunch for us both. You got time to eat?"

"I do have time, but I'm sorry King sent you. I'm sure you have plenty to do today without babysitting me."

She waves me off as she sets the bag on the counter and starts unloading everything. "Please, I'm just giving my brother shit. I wanted to come see you. You don't know how excited I am to have a sister."

I smile at her, but it doesn't quite reach my eyes. I'm happy to have a sister too, but a part of me wonders how long this is going to last. His brothers and Chrissy have all seemed to accept me, and for the first time last night, I felt what it was like to be a part of a family. "I'm excited to have a sister too."

Chrissy takes out the last container. "Yeah, and not just any sister… I'm a sister that has brought you a slice of the famous apple cinnamon Blaze cake."

My mouth drops open. "You didn't."

She opens the container and inhales it and then sticks it under my nose. "I did. You want to eat this first?"

I hold up a finger. "Okay, one bite."

We each take a spoon, and as we scoop up a huge bite for each of us, we cackle because we think we're funny. Nope, no little bite for us.

We start with the cake and then we go to the chicken salads. There's no pause in the conversation, and I appreciate how easy it is to talk to Chrissy. She tells me about her job as a nurse at the hospital in Jasper, and I tell her stories about my modeling career. My cheeks hurt from smiling so much.

Chrissy wipes her mouth with the napkin. "I can't believe my brother didn't send Callan with you today."

I roll my eyes like I'm frustrated, but the truth is, I appreciate how protective he is with me. "I had to convince him that I was okay. This is exactly five miles from the house, and it's Whiskey Run. He keeps saying he's going to hire me a full-time driver, but I told him it would be such a waste of money."

Chrissy shrugs and searches my eyes. "I get it, I do. You're independent, but that's just the way that King shows how he cares for someone. He's not big on affection or things like that… so this is how you know he cares for you. He looks out for the people he loves."

Her words do something to me, and I nod my head. She doesn't know that this is fake and that her brother doesn't love me. "Okay."

We finish eating, and I take her on a tour of the

community center before telling her all the plans. We're back to the front when my phone rings, and I hold it up. "It's King."

She rolls her eyes. "Well, I'll go so you two lovebirds can talk. See you soon, sis."

"See you soon. Thank you for lunch. My treat next time."

She points at me as she's walking out the door. "I'll hold you to it. Tell my brother I did my job and checked in on his wife. See you!"

I'm waving at her as I answer my phone. "Hey, husband."

His voice is husky. "Oh I like you answering the phone that way."

I giggle. "Chrissy just left. She fed me and kept me company. You do know I don't need a babysitter, right?"

There's some noise in the background, and it's obvious his office is busy, but he doesn't seem to care. "I know you don't. I just hate for you to be there by yourself all day, that's all. Is that okay?"

I sigh because how can I not completely fall in love with him? "Yeah, it's okay."

"Good. Do you have plans tonight?"

My heart rate picks up. "Nope. No plans."

"Good. I have something special planned. Can you be ready by six?"

I look at the clock on my phone and see it's only two o'clock. "I sure can."

"Okay, I need to go, but I'll see you at the house at six."

"I'll be ready," I promise.

His voice drops. "Bye, wife."

A thrill goes through me. "Bye, husband."

As soon as he hangs up, I try to imagine what he could have planned. I am at a standstill for the community center, so I can take the rest of the day off and go home to get ready.

As soon as I make the decision, I pack up my things, throw my bag over my shoulder, lock up, and hustle out of the building. If I go home now, I'll have more than enough time to shower, curl my hair, and get ready for tonight.

As I'm walking to my car, someone hollers at me, "Miss. Excuse me, miss."

I turn, and as soon as I do, a man on a skateboard flies by and knocks me to the ground. I go sprawling face first. Jarred, I lay here for a minute, and the man that was hollering at me comes next to me. "Are you okay, miss?"

I roll to my back and look up at him. "Yeah, I

think so."

He helps me up, and I'm so out of it, he has to practically drag me to my feet and hold on to me. He's hovering over me, and I'm gripping on to him because I'm afraid my legs are going to buckle. I can feel the road rash on my knees and my hands.

"Thank you," I murmur. The man holds on to me and asks over and over if I'm okay. When I get my bearings, I try to pull from his arms, but he's reluctant to let me go. "Are you sure you're okay?"

I nod and force a smile to my face. "I'm okay. Thank you."

He stands next to me for a few minutes as I try to catch my breath. We both inspect my knees and my hands, which are bleeding. "Those are nasty cuts. Are you sure I can't help you?"

"No, I'm going home. I can take care of them there."

After the man finally walks away, I take a good look at my knees and my hands, and it's not pretty. I take a step toward my car and wince at the pain in my ankle. It's bearable, but it hurts. I hobble toward my car, and the whole way, I'm refusing to let this upset me. King has a date night planned, and I'm not going to let anything ruin it. I'll clean my cuts up and be good as new.

28

KING

"CAN you go over the list one more time? I want to make sure I didn't miss anything."

My assistant Rachel taps her pencil on the notebook she's holding. "Flowers, check. Dinner, check. Gift, check." She looks up at me. "Have you prepared what you're going to say, or are you going to wing it?"

I nod. "I know what I'm going to say."

Rachel stands up. "Well, I think you're good then. Everything is perfect, and she's going to love it. I really like her. She was so nice the day she was in here, and you seem happier, which makes working here nicer."

I roll my eyes with a chuckle. "You're just happy I'm not in the office as much."

"Yeah, that definitely helps." She laughs at her own joke and then walks over to the door. "No, seriously, it's good to see you like this. Don't screw it up."

There's not many people I would let talk to me like that, but Rachel is one of them. She's been with me for almost twenty years, and she's always been a say it like it is kind of person. "I don't plan to. I'm going to get out of here soon. You can head out whenever."

She puts her hand over her heart. "Oh, another short day. My husband is not going to know what to think with me coming home early all the time. "

It's my turn to laugh. "Henry loves it, and I know he does."

Rachel laughs and then before she gets out the office, she slaps her hand on the door. "Shoot, I almost forgot. Becca wanted to see you before you left today."

I nod as I start gathering papers to put in my briefcase. "Can you schedule something with her in the morning? I was hoping to get out a little early."

"I'll tell her. Have a good night, boss."

I tell her the same, and it's only when I'm in the quiet of my office that I reflect on what I'm about to do. I only told Haven that I had a special night planned, leaving her to imagine what's going on. I am a little nervous, but I'd be even more nervous if I did nothing. These last few weeks with Haven have been the best of my life. It seems like forever I've looked for somewhere I fit in and someone I felt at home with. Hell, I'm a millionaire. I have the nice home, the car, the business, the reputation—I thought I had it all. It wasn't until I met Haven that I realized none of those other things matter. The only thing that matters to me is her. I can't imagine my life without her in it.

I messed up by letting her think this was some kind of fake arrangement and we were doing it just to have kids and to save my reputation. Hell, I need to fix it and make sure she knows how much she means to me and how much I need her in my life permanently. I'm going to tell her how I feel. I'm pretty sure she feels the same way too, but I'm not going to pressure her. Of course, I want her to love me back, but I'll wait for her.

I pull out my phone and look at the picture taken the other night at dinner. Chrissy took it, and as I scroll the pictures, it's obvious how much Chrissy and my brothers already love my wife. She fits right in with our self-made family, and I want more nights like that one. I want forever with Haven.

While I have my phone out, I shoot her a text. "I'll see you soon, wife. I'm leaving early."

She sends me a picture of herself, sitting on our bed. It's innocent enough, she's fully clothed, but it still takes my imagination on a loop. The text she sent with it says, "I'm already home waiting for you, husband."

I look at my clock, and it's almost four. I told Haven I'd pick her up at six, but I can't wait another second to ask her to be mine... for real this time.

I ride the elevator down, letting Callan know I'm on the way.

I'm almost to my car when my marketing manager, Becca, runs to catch up with me. "Sir... Ridge... can I have a moment please?"

I look at my watch impatiently. "I need to be somewhere. Can this wait until the morning?"

She's holding a manila envelope. "I think you'll want to see this, sir. It just came by courier."

Out of patience, I give my briefcase to Callan. "Keep the car running. I'll be there in a minute."

I take the envelope from Becca, and she watches as I open it. It's not uncommon for couriers to bring over papers that need to be signed, but I'm surprised when I pull out pictures. Instantly, all I see is red. Image after image of Haven... my wife... in another man's arms.

He's touching her, holding her, smiling at her, and she is letting him. I get to the last picture, and he has his arms around her, and she's looking at him with a big smile on her face. It's almost too intimate to even look at.

Without another word to Becca, I turn on my heel and make my way to the car.

"Home," I say to Callan and then close off the partition between us. Everything was perfect. I had a whole night planned, and I was going to tell Haven I love her. And now I find out it's all a big sham.

The drive home is thirty minutes, and I think that's good so I can calm myself down, but it does the opposite. The more I think about another man touching Haven, the more upset I become.

I'm barely hanging on when we pull into the driveway. "Thanks, Callan. I won't be needing you anymore tonight."

I get out of the car with a slam of the door and then walk up to my house.

As soon as I walk inside, I see Haven. She's all

dressed up with a smile on her face. She's sitting at the barstool, her phone sitting in front of her, and she exclaims, "You're home."

I drop the manilla folder on the counter and go straight to the liquor cabinet. I maybe drink one time a year, but I'd say this occasion calls for it.

"Hello, wife," I say tersely.

"What's wrong?"

I point at the manila folder. "I got that today. It was interesting."

She points at the folder. "What is it?"

I take a shot of the whiskey and slam the glass down on the counter with a thud. I spit the words out at her. "Pictures… of you with your boyfriend."

"What?" she asks, shaking her head. "I don't have a boyfriend. You're talking nonsense, King. What is that?"

I laugh, and even to me it sounds maniacal, but I feel like that right now. "Right, like you don't know. Go ahead, look at it."

29

HAVEN

FROM THE MOMENT King walked in the door, I knew something was up. This is not the same man that gave me two orgasms this morning before he'd even let me out of bed. He's angry, and I've never seen him this way before.

As I reach for the envelope, he puts his hands on the counter top and leans on them. "What was your plan here, Haven? Get me to marry you and what, wait it out, get a divorce, and run off with the money?"

"Divorce?" I stutter.

He laughs again, but it's not a happy laugh. "I mean, you've put in a lot of effort into this. Even fucking me. My question is, how did you know? How did you know I'd fall for it? I mean, don't get me wrong, your pussy is good… But I've had better."

My mouth drops, and I stare at my husband in shock. To go from the excitement I felt only moments ago to this is like being on a roller coaster that has gone off the rails. I'm completely lost on why—or even how—he could talk to me this way. "I don't know what you're talking about."

"Look at the pictures and then tell me you don't know what I'm talking about. You've lied to me this whole time, Haven, and I fell for it."

My hands are shaking as I pull open the tab on the envelope. Slowly, I pull out the pictures. One by one, I lay them on the counter and stare at them. I keep wiping at the tears that are rolling down my face, but I don't say anything.

It's the man from today. The one that helped me after I fell.

I could explain this easily—heck, I have the cuts on my hands and knees to prove it, but as I raise my head and look into King's eyes, I know I'd be wasting my time. "You really believe I'd do something like that to you? You think…" I shudder. "You think I'd cheat on you?"

He waves his hand over the pictures. "Are you going to explain?"

I repeat the question. "You truly believe that I would lie to you… that I would cheat on you?"

He smacks his hand on the countertop. "No, Haven, I wouldn't have thought that, but luckily someone thought they should send me these pictures and show me exactly what kind of woman I married. I'm a fool… a damn fool."

My heart feels like it's ripping in my chest. "You are a fool, King."

I get up from the stool I'm sitting on and try not to wince when I put my weight on my ankle. With a slight limp I walk from the room, but King follows me.

"Where do you think you're going? This isn't over. I'm still talking to you."

As calm as I can, I tell him, "Well, I'm done talking to you."

He follows me up the steps. "What's wrong with you? Why are you limping?"

I turn on him, and for the first time, I raise my voice to him. "Don't. Just don't. You don't care, so don't act like you do."

I try to move faster, ignoring the pain shooting in my ankle. I grab my suitcase from the closet and start throwing things in the bag. He's leaning against the door jamb, arms crossed over his chest and staring at me with hatred.

I disappear into the bathroom, and whatever I can grab in my two hands, I pick up. The rest I can just buy later. I dump it into my bag, and it's all so haphazard, I struggle getting it zipped up.

"Where do you think you're going?"

I wipe the stupid tears from my face. "I'm leaving."

I yank the bag off the bed onto the floor and start to roll it. As I walk next to him to get out the door, he puts his hand up on the door frame to block me. "If you're pregnant, that's my kid too. I have a right to know."

I can't even look at him. "I wouldn't keep your child from you, King. Can you please just let me go?"

"Of course, I'd want a paternity test because how do we know whose kid it really is?"

I lean over because it feels like I've been kicked in the gut. "Please… I need to leave."

He lifts his arm and lets me go. I get to the top of the stairs and struggle with the bag on the staircase. I get a few steps down when King calls my name. "Haven."

I stop, a part of me hoping he's going to say he

realized he's made a mistake. That he was wrong and that he loves me, but what actually comes out of his mouth is nothing like that. "You played your part well. I actually thought I'd fallen in love with you. That's what I was coming to tell you. That's what I had planned for tonight. I'm a fuckin' fool."

I clench my eyes shut and grip onto the banister of the stairs to stop from falling. Unable to take another second, I toss the suitcase the remainder of the way down the steps. I hobble down after it and then grab my keys and purse by the front door. I walk out without looking back once.

I haphazardly throw everything into my car and pull out of the driveway. It's not until I'm on the road that I let the tears flow, and as soon as they start to flow, I can't stop it. My body wracks with the force of my sobs. I keep driving, but I can't see anything. I wipe at my eyes, but it's only a momentary fix. I can't continue like this.

I pull into the driveway of Chrissy's house and throw my car into park. As I sit here, I let it all out. My throat is raw, my eyes are already swollen, and my heart is completely shattered. I don't realize anyone is here until my car door flies open. "Haven, what is it? What's wrong? Are you okay?"

Oh God. I cry even harder as Chrissy rubs my

back. "Haven, talk to me, you're freaking me out. What's wrong? Is it King? Is he okay?"

I suck in a deep breath and nod. "He's fine. I'm sorry. I couldn't see the road, and I just pulled in here. I shouldn't be here. I need to go."

She reaches in and grabs the steering wheel. "You one hundred percent should be here. Come on, get out. You're coming inside."

I can't look at her. "Chrissy, I'm fine. I promise."

She's incredulous. "You're not fine. Now get out of the car."

I get out of the car, and almost instantly Chrissy notices my limp. "What happened to you, sis?"

I start to cry again when she calls me sis and I don't stop until I'm inside, sitting on the couch.

Chrissy sits next to me. "Talk to me."

I inhale slowly and wipe at my eyes. I know I'm a mess. "King and I are over."

Chrissy sits back, stunned. "What?"

My breath shudders. "Yeah, uh, he thinks I cheated on him. He thinks that I planned all this to… get his money… I don't know."

"Well, that's stupid. Anyone that has seen you two together can see you love him."

I start to cry again. Yeah, I love him. Even now

with every hateful thing he said, I still love him. "Well, it doesn't matter how I feel about him… It's over."

She's shaking her head, "Explain to me what happened. I don't understand."

Slowly, I start to explain. "I really don't know. He showed up with pictures of me and some man, but it's not what it looks like. I fell today outside the community center, and the guy was helping me up. I twisted my ankle, cut up my knees and hands."

I hold them out for her to inspect, and she winces. "Oh my God, Haven. That looks horrible."

"It's okay. Trust me, it's the least of my worries."

She gets up and walks out of the room, but she keeps talking as she goes. "Well, it shouldn't be. You don't want that to get infected."

She's back shortly and sits down on the coffee table in front of me. "Let me clean it out for you."

I feel numb as she works on my knees and my hands. Neither one of us says a word, but my mind is racing the whole entire time.

When she has me bandaged up, she lifts my foot up and removes my shoes. She tilts my foot different directions. "Does this hurt? What about this?"

I wince but shake my head. "It's fine."

She gently places my foot on the floor. "It's sprained. I think I have a brace around here for when you get up and walk, but let's get it propped up and ice it for now."

"No! I mean, thank you, Chrissy. Really, this means a lot to me, but I need to go. Thanks for cleaning me up… but I should go."

She's not listening, though. "You're not leaving. You're staying right here. I'm going to get the spare room set up, and you're going to stay here with me."

"I can't. I'm not going to come between you and your brother. I need to go."

She throws her hands up in the air. "My brother needs to get his head out of his ass. I should have known he'd find a way to fuck this up. Look, I'm not making excuses for him. King is our big brother, and for years he's the one that took care of all of us. I wouldn't have been able to go to school if it wasn't for him. Holden wouldn't be playing in the big leagues, Dom, Ledger, and Gabe… well you get my drift. But he's been through hell, Haven. His mom didn't have anything to do with him until he made some kind of big list after he made his first million from building skyscrapers. I mean, the women have come out of the woodwork to try to trick him into relationships… but that's no excuse. He should know you and know you're not like that."

I'm shaking my head, ready to get up and leave, but Chrissy stops me. "Please stay. Do this for me. I'll worry about you if you leave."

"But…"

"Please, Haven."

I nod. "Okay. One night and then I'll get out of your hair. I gave up my apartment, but I bet it hasn't been rented. I'll leave in the morning."

"You're not in my hair, and you'll hurt my feelings if you leave. I'll get you some clothes to put on and then I'll help you get settled."

"My bag is in the car. I can get it."

"I'll get it. I'll be right back."

She's out the front door before I can talk her out of it. As soon as she's gone, I fall back on the couch and throw my arm over my face. My head is killing me, my ankle is throbbing, and I feel sick to my stomach. I close my eyes and try to clear my head because if I start thinking about my husband and my disaster of a marriage, I'm going to start crying again.

30

______

KING

MY HEAD IS POUNDING.

I lift my head off my desk, and everything is blurry. I rub at my eyes and am surprised that the pounding is not actually in my head, but at my front door. Before I can get up, I hear my brother Holden hollering my name.

Fuck. I'm not in the mood for this right now. If I'm quiet, will he go away? I lay my head back on the desk, and right in front of me is the empty ⅕ bottle of Blaze whiskey that I drank last night.

I clench my eyes as it all starts to come back to me. It's all fake. She played me, and I fell for it.

"What the fuck, King?" Holden says as he falls down in the chair opposite me.

"Please… just leave me alone."

He picks up the empty bottle, shakes it, and sets it down. "You don't drink, brother."

I try to raise my head, but the room starts to spin, and so I lay my cheek back down on the desk. "I did last night."

"You're an idiot, you know that, right?"

I roll my eyes and groan at the pain that shoots in my head. "Shouldn't you be throwing a ball somewhere or something?"

"Yeah, I have to head out for a five-day series, but I wanted to come and help you get your head out of your ass before I go."

"Fuck you," I groan.

He just laughs. "So uh, hear me out. Sis called me, and just a note, she's not happy with you at all. I've never seen her this mad."

I close my eyes. I hate to piss off my sister, and I'm sure by now Haven has told her lies about what's happened.

Holden blows out a breath. "Anyway, I went and talked to Haven—"

I finally raise my head up. "Where is she?"

Instead of answering, he says, "Anyway, I talked to her and she told me about the pictures."

I hold my head in my hands. "Did she tell you she broke my heart? That she's with another man?"

I grab one of the pictures and shove it toward him. "See.. Here's proof."

He rolls his chair closer to the desk and picks up the picture that I've stared at all night. "Hhhmmm… good picture, but I saw it on video."

I groan. "On video? Of course it's on video. I can't watch it… just kill me now."

"For a millionaire, you're really dumb, King."

I don't have it in me to argue with him.

"Anyway, after talking to Haven, I then talked to Callan and had him pull the video footage outside of the community center."

He pauses, and I just sit here, concentrating on breathing without the room spinning.

"The video shows two men talking outside. Then Haven comes out, and one of the men knocks her to the ground, and the other man picks her up."

I raise my eyes to look at him, not believing what I'm hearing. "What did you just say?"

"Two men—"

I cut him off. "Someone knocked her to the ground? Someone hurt her?"

"Fuck, you look like death. Your eyes look like they're bleeding."

"So she wasn't with another man."

He looks at me worriedly. "No, man. How did

you miss her skinned-up knees and hands and her sprained ankle? She was hurt."

"Who did it? Who hurt her?"

"Callan's been working on it all night. He's identified the two men and the person that hired them."

I shoot out of my seat and sway on my feet. I lean over on my desk so I can stay upright. "Someone hired them to hurt her?"

"Becca Archer, your marketing manager, hired them so she could get pictures of her with someone else."

"But—"

He cuts me off. "Haven didn't do anything wrong, King."

"Someone hurt her?"

Holden winces. "Trust me, brother. No one has hurt her more than you did."

"What have I done?"

He crosses his arms over his chest and stares at me. "You did what you always do. At the first opportunity, you pushed her away before you could give her a chance to explain. The only difference is, she didn't deserve it. That girl is so fuckin' in love with you…"

He stops talking, letting his voice trail off, and I

think back on everything I said to her. As it replays in my head, I panic. God, I hurt her. I intentionally tried to hurt her because I thought she betrayed me. I said things I didn't mean. I stumble out of the room and up the stairs. Holden follows me, and as soon as I get upstairs, I strip down and step into the ice cold shower.

"Fuck, King, how about a warning? The last thing I want to see is your ass right now."

I stand under the spray and let it hit me in the face. Holden continues to talk from the other room. "Callan is just waiting on your direction. He assumed you'd want to fire Becca. You just need to give him the word."

"Fire her," I croak.

As soon as I'm out of the shower, I walk naked into the bedroom, and Holden jumps up from the end of the bed. "What the fuck, brother? I don't want to see your dick either."

I start yanking clothes out of my drawers and get dressed. "Where is she? Where's Haven?"

"She was crying so hard when she left here, Chrissy found her outside her house."

It's like a knife to my heart. I did that to her. "Can you drop me off?"

He nods, and I'm walking downstairs and out

the door without another word between us. Holden drives me down the block and pulls into Chrissy's driveway. "She doesn't want to see you."

I can't say I blame her. I can't stand myself right now either. "I have to make this right."

He blows out a breath. "I gotta go. I have to be in North Carolina tonight, and the plane's leaving soon."

"Thanks, brother. For everything."

I get out and make my way up to Chrissy's front door. My sister answers, and she looks at me angrily. "She doesn't want to see you… I don't want to see you either." She starts to shut the door, but I put my foot out to stop her.

"Please, Chrissy. I need to talk to her."

When she doesn't open the door any farther, I tell her, "I'm not leaving here until I see her."

She finally opens the door and stands to the side so I can go in. "Fix this, King. She's in the spare bedroom at the back of the house."

I nod and don't waste any time walking down the hall to where Haven is. I knock on the open door and push it open, letting out a breath when I see her sitting on the bed. She's sitting cross-legged with a notebook in her lap. When she looks up at me, I notice her eyes are swollen and red. Fuck, I did that to her.

Slowly, I walk into the bedroom. She tenses and pleads with me, "Please, King. I can't do this."

"I'm sorry."

"You're sorry?" she asks.

I nod and move closer to her. I don't stop until I'm standing next to where she's sitting on the bed. "Yeah, I'm sorry. I'm sorry for doubting you, for the awful things I said to you, for not trusting you."

She lets out a frustrated breath and scoots away, putting some distance between us. "King—"

I move and sit down on the edge of the bed. "I'm sorry that I wasn't there to protect you..."

31

___

HAVEN

I STILL CAN'T BELIEVE that Chrissy told me that I was knocked down on purpose and why the pictures were taken. "So you know what happened?"

He winces. "I do now. I should have asked you instead of accusing you, Haven."

Yeah, he should have. But it's too late now. "Actually, it's probably a good thing this happened." I've thought about it all night, and I realize that I'd set myself up for failure. I was in a marriage that was over before it even began. I don't know why I thought I could do it. Of course, I would fall in love with him. So it's better this way... better now before there's a kid involved.

He leans toward me. I've kept my eyes off him,

but now that I look at him, I realize he looks like he didn't get any sleep last night. His eyes are bloodshot. I point to his face. "Are you all right?"

He runs his hand across his face. "Am I all right? God, don't ask me that. I don't know if I'll ever be all right again. I hate myself for how I treated you, peaches. I drank until I blacked out last night."

I shift, putting more distance between us, but he moves closer. "Are you okay?" He reaches out to caress my knee, and I jerk away from his touch. I hold my hands up so he can see the scratches on them. "I'm fine. Your sister cleaned out my cuts and got me a brace for my ankle."

He looks devastated, and I hate that I'm worried about him. We've talked about it, and he's told me that he never drinks because he once had a foster parent that would drink and take out his anger on the kids. It kills me to know he resorted to drinking last night.

But even though I feel for him, I have to have some self-preservation. "Like I said, it's probably good this has happened, King. We are messed up. We're two people that are messed up. This isn't going to work, and it doesn't matter since it's all fake anyway. You don't trust me..."

I let my voice trail off as emotion overcomes me. I shudder a breath to try and pull myself together. "We need to end this now before it gets out of hand and someone gets hurt."

"Haven, listen to me. I don't know how to explain it. I saw you with another man's arms around you. I went crazy."

I interrupt him. I can't look at him, so I'm picking at the thread on the bed cover. "And you thought I slept with you one night and then went to another man. I would never do that. You thought I was after your money, and that's not who I am. I don't care about your money."

"I know that. I know that's not who you are. I'm sorry, Haven."

"You said that."

He reaches for me, putting his hand on my knee again and tracing his thumb back and forth on my skin. I'm weak because even now I crave his touch. I watch his hand, and after a minute, I pull my leg away. "Listen, so I talked to Chrissy. I'm going to stay here—"

"No, you're going to stay at our home, with me."

"I can't, King. I can't stay there."

He reaches for me, grabbing my hands and

pulling them to his chest. "Please, I'm begging you, Haven. Stay at our house."

I pull from his hold and stand up on the opposite side of the bed. He stands up, and we face off against each other. I cross my arms over my chest. "I will stay at your house until I know I'm not pregnant. In the meantime, I'll be looking for an apartment. I called this morning, and mine had already been rented. I'll hire someone to finish the community center."

"The community center is yours, Haven."

I smile wistfully. "At one time, I believed that. But it's not any more mine than you are, King."

He's shaking his head. "But I am yours. I'm your husband, Haven."

I shake my head. "And we'll start proceedings for the divorce." I raise my hand up, knowing what he's about to say. "I don't want any money… I just want this to be over. I need to get on with my life."

"We're not getting a divorce."

God, this hurts. "I can't stay with you, King. Not now."

He looks lost. I wait for him to argue with me or tell me no, but he surprises me. "So you're coming home?"

"I'll stay there—in the guest room—until I get

everything settled. As soon as I find a place to live, I'm leaving."

He doesn't answer me. He goes over to the corner of the room where my suitcase is lying open, and he closes it and zips it up. He picks it up and then rolls it to the door. "I'm going to take this out to your car. I'll be back to help you."

He disappears, and I go over to where my shoes are and slide them on. I hobble to the front door where Chrissy is waiting for me. "You okay?"

Instead of answering her, I blow out a breath. Overwhelmed doesn't cover it, so I say nothing.

She opens her arms, and I step into them, letting her hug me. If nothing else, my time with King has opened me up to touch… at least with his family. "Thank you for everything."

She whispers into my ear, "You'll always be my sister, Haven."

I shudder a breath, and she continues. "I know it's a lot to ask. I know he hurt you, but I also know that it's because he's spent all his life being hurt, Haven. It's not right… he didn't handle it right… but I hope you let him make it up to you."

I don't know what to say to her, so I just nod my head. She hugs me one more time, and I meet King on the front porch.

He tries to help me, but I shake my head. "I got it. I'm good."

He sighs but doesn't argue with me. He opens the passenger side of my car and then gets in the driver's seat. He doesn't talk the whole way there, and I can't help but wonder if I'm making the worst decision by going home with him.

I glance over at him and take in his disheveled look. I've never seen King look like he does right now.

As we pull into the driveway and park, I'm out of the car before King can come around and open my door. I let him grab my suitcase as I walk up the porch to the house. I'm about to disappear up the stairs to my room when he stops me. "Haven, wait. Please."

I stop with one hand on the railing. "What is it, King?"

"I'm sorry I hurt you. I'm sorry that I looked at those pictures and thought what I did instead of asking you about them. I'm sorry that those men got to you and I didn't protect you. I'm sorry for how I acted and how I made you feel. I was wrong, and I know I don't deserve it, but I'm asking you— I'm begging you—to give me a chance to make this up to you."

My hand tightens on the banister. Right now, I feel like I can't even function, and all I want to do is go to bed and stay there for a week. Without turning around and looking at him, I tell him the truth. "I don't know if I can do that… I'm going to lie down."

I continue up the steps, and he doesn't try to stop me. As I lie down on the bed, I try to ignore the part of me that wants to run to King and make it all okay.

32
___

KING

I'M PRETTY SURE this is what going crazy feels like.

The fun, happy Haven is gone, and it kills me what I've done to her.

Yesterday, she spent all day in bed. I brought her food, cleaned and changed the bandages on her cuts, and then hovered nearby, hoping to just get a glance at her. She slept in the spare bedroom, and I couldn't stand it, so after she went to sleep, I went in and slept on the chair in the corner of her room.

This morning, she got up to go to the community center, and I had Callan drive us here. This place usually brings her so much joy, but it's like the light has gone out of her. I ask Callan to grab us breakfast from the Glaze Bakery downtown, and as soon as he leaves, I ask Haven, "What's the plan for today?"

She's looking at the notebook in her hands. "I have some interviews set up for an assistant, but while we're interviewing them, we can see what we think of them as the manager too."

Fuck, she's determined to move on from me.

She continues, "I hired the painters, and they're supposed to start today. Next week, the furniture is getting moved in. This afternoon, I'm going to look at an apartment, but it's right down the road, so I can walk."

When I don't say anything, she finally looks up from her notepad. "You know it's crazy for you to hang out here all day. You have a company to run."

I stuff my hands in my pockets because its either that or I'm going to be reaching for her. "The two men have been tracked down and taken care of. Becca's been fired, and I don't think she'll bother you, but I'm not chancing it."

"So what? You're just going to hang out here all day, every day? That doesn't make sense. Hire someone so you can get to work."

"You don't get it, Haven. I can't even think about work. I had a meeting today. A prospect for a twenty-five million dollar project, and I canceled. I don't care about anything right now except making things right between me and you."

She looks down, and it kills me that she can't look at me. "King, that's crazy, you know that, right?"

I shrug and tell her honestly, "I sort of feel like I'm going crazy. I miss you… I miss us."

Haven takes a deep breath. Something is weighing on her, and finally she says something. "What is it with you and her?"

I don't understand. "Me and who?"

"Becca… your manager."

"She was my marketing manager."

Haven rolls her eyes. "I know that. I'm asking if she was your girlfriend. Were you sleeping with her?"

"No!" I exclaim. Fuck, is that what she thinks? "No and no. She was not my girlfriend, and I've never slept with her."

I barely get the words out and Haven lets out the breath she's holding.

"So she did this… why? Because she was into you?"

I cringe just knowing what I let that woman do and how I let her come between Haven and me.

"She was flirty, but I never encouraged her, and I never expected this."

She shifts her weight and winces when she puts pressure on her ankle. "Here," I tell her, pushing a chair toward her. She sits down, and I pull up the other chair to sit next to her.

She's staring at the ground, her notepad, hell everywhere except at me. "Look at me, Haven. Please."

She finally lifts her pretty blues to mine, and it kills me when I see what's reflected back at me. I hurt her and am still hurting her.

"What can I do to help you today?"

She shakes her head. "King."

I reach over and wrap my hand around hers. She doesn't pull away, and the fact she doesn't is huge. "You can ask me for anything, Haven. And I'd give it to you."

She opens her mouth, but I stop her. "You can ask me for anything, but you need to know that there's some things I can't—I won't—do. I won't let you leave me. I won't let you move into some apartment. I won't let you end this."

"But..." she starts, and this time, her voice trails off.

"I will give you space, and I will give you time… but I won't let you go. I can't."

The front door opens, and Callan comes walking in with a bag and tray of drinks. He sets them on the counter. "Here you go. You need anything else, King?"

"No. That's it. Thank you."

Instead of leaving, Callan turns to Haven. "And you? Do you need anything, Haven?"

She seems surprised, but I'm not. Callan was pissed about the footage of the man pushing her down. She shakes her head. "I'm good. Thank you for the coffee, Callan."

"You're welcome."

He walks back out, and I set the coffee and the pastry down in front of her.

She looks at me. "I had to cancel my modeling jobs for the next two weeks. If they were photoshoots, they could just photoshop the cuts, but they're runway shows, and no one wants to see this."

Shit. Another thing I've taken from her. "I'm sorry, Haven."

She shrugs. "It's okay, actually. There's a lot to do here, so I'll be able to stay busy. Hopefully, I can get everything tied up in the next two weeks."

I fucked up so badly, and I'm not sure if I'm going to be able to fix it. I would give anything to have her look at me the way she did the other day. Now she's so guarded, I'm not sure if she's ever going to let me in.

33

HAVEN

"YOU GOING to hide out in here all night?"

I look at King leaning against my bedroom door, and a heat comes over me. I've been with him all day. He's been super attentive, he's touched me at every turn. It's almost as if he's trying to remind me that I like his touch. What he doesn't know is that I've gone beyond liking his touch; I crave it now. Even to the point where I imagine it, dream it, and think about it all day long.

I'm still hurt, and it kills me to know that I may never be able to get over it. "I'm not hiding out."

He comes into the room and sits down on the bed, next to my hip. "You are hiding out. You're retreating and pulling back from me."

I inhale and suck in his manly scent. How am I supposed to think straight when he looks and smells the way he does? This is not fair. "I have to, King."

He puts a hand on my knee. His finger traces circles on my bare skin, causing goosebumps. "Because I have to protect myself. This will be over soon."

He shakes his head. "If you think I'm going to let you leave me—"

I cut him off with a laugh. "Don't worry. I'm not taking any of your money when I go."

His jaw tightens as he stares at me. "I'm not worried about you leaving with my money."

I jut my chin at him. "Then what? Why can't you just let me go?"

He puts his hand to his chest. "My heart, peaches. I can't let you leave because you'd be taking my heart with you. I love you, Haven. I know it's no excuse, but that's why I lost it when I saw those pictures. I couldn't lose you. I'm sorry, and I promise, if you'll let me, I'll spend the rest of my life making it up to you."

"King—"

He leans toward me. "I've only ever said those words to my brothers and my sister. I know how important they are, and I know what they mean. I love you, Haven. None of this is fake. It's real to me. Yes, I want to have kids, but I want to have kids with you. I want to spend my life showing you how beautiful and special you are. I want you to have everything you want out of life because you deserve it. I know I fucked up, and I know…"

I stop him this time because I need to hear it again. "Say it again."

He smiles at me. "I love you, Haven Beckett. Today and forever, I love you."

I lean forward. My heart is practically beating out of my chest. "Now kiss me."

His whole body shudders, and he moans in relief. He wastes no time and pulls me against him as he kisses me as if he can't bear the thought of losing me. The kiss is a gnashing of our lips, tongues, and teeth. It's like we can't get close enough.

I pull back, and his hands dig into my hips, not letting me go far. "I need you, King. Please. Now."

He stands up and discards the clothes he's wearing while I lie back and struggle to do the same. I have my panties around my ankles, and he strips them away before lying down on top of me.

"Sorry, I'm heavy," he says, trying to put his weight on his arms.

I hold on to him. "No, don't go. I want to be close to you."

I wrap myself around him, holding him close and breathing him in. I can't get enough of him, and I'm overwhelmed by the last few days.

He holds on to me like he doesn't want to let me go. "What do you need, peaches? Whatever it is—"

I raise my head to look at him. "You… I just need you."

He nods. "I'm yours."

I let my hand trail between us, and I wrap it around his hard girth. His hips push him farther into my hand, and he groans. We both need this. I'm so ready for him, I open my legs, letting his body fit against me.

His hard cock sits at my entrance, but he doesn't take me. His hands are everywhere. He's touching and tasting me until I'm practically begging him to take me.

"Please, King."

"Look at me," he demands.

I don't raise my eyes, though. I know what he's going to see on my face if I do, and it scares me. I've been hurt my whole life, but King could obliterate me. Letting my guard down scares the hell out of me.

He rolls to his back, taking me with him, and when we stop, I'm spread-eagle on top of him. His hands go to my face, and he holds me so that I have no choice but look at him.

"I love you, Haven."

"But what if you change your mind? What if—"

"I love you, Haven. Forever I will love you, and if it takes me the rest of our lives to convince you, I'm happy to do it. I can't lose you... I will never lose you."

My heart starts to race, and I know I need to be brave here. "I love you, King. I want you to know, I love you... please don't hurt me. I won't survive it."

"Oh baby," he says, pulling me down so he can kiss me. Our lips meet in a perfect symphony, and I get lost in the kiss.

His hands travel down my body, and he grabs my hips, dragging me across his erection. His lips pop off mine. "Ride me, peaches."

I raise up, and he positions himself at my core. Slowly, I impale myself on him. With my eyes clenched close, I start to move, riding him.

"Haven, baby, look at me."

I stare at him as I rise and lower over him.

Looking into his eyes takes our lovemaking to a whole other level. He meets me thrust for thrust. "I love you, my wife."

As I grind my clit against him, I moan. "I love you too, my husband."

34

HAVEN

I STRETCH and moan as the muscles that I didn't even know I had ache. It's a good kind of hurt and instantly I think of last night in King's arms.

I turn to King's side of the bed and open my eyes, expecting to see my husband. When I find the bed empty, I sit up in surprise, looking around the room.

He's gone. I listen to the quiet house, wondering if he's here or not, but I don't hear anything. I sit up to reach for my phone on the nightstand and see the letter sitting on top of it.

I grab it and start to read. *Hey wife, I'm sorry I left early this morning but I didn't want to wake you. Take your time but when you're ready, come to the community center, I have a surprise for you. Callan is waiting for you in the car. Love you. King.*

I read the note again and then look at the time on my phone. It's almost ten a.m. I get up and run to the window, and sure enough, Callan is sitting in the driveway. I send him a text. I'll be down in twenty.

Callan likes the text, and I rush through showering and getting ready for the day. I'm a little nervous about the surprise, but I'm excited too. I'm hoping after last night, this all works out. I'm not a fool. I know it's not always going to be easy, but I do hope whatever happens, we work through it all together.

"Morning," I say to Callan as he holds the back door open for me.

"Morning, Mrs. Beckett."

I almost ask him to call me Haven, but I like hearing my married name.

It only takes a few minutes to get to the community center, and when we get there, there's a crowd outside.

I find my husband in the middle of all of them, and he pulls me into his arms. "Morning, peaches."

He kisses me until I'm breathless, but I don't object, even though people are surrounding us.

I pat his chest. "Morning, King."

He points up at the building, and there's a draped curtain over it. "This is your surprise. I hope you love it."

"You didn't have to get me anything, King, but I'm sure whatever it is, I'm going to love it."

The small crowd is looking between King and the sign on the building, and he draws me into his arms. "Everyone, since you're here, we want you to be the first to see the name of the new community center. The community center has been in the works for years, but it's only since Haven got involved that it's coming to fruition. I'm lucky that my wife is as passionate as she is when it comes to serving the community and saving children. My wife is…" He chokes up and shakes his head to get composure. "My wife is everything to me, and she's going to do amazing things here." He turns to me and puts his hands on my cheeks. "I love you, Haven Beckett. And I'm so proud that you're my wife. May I present to you… Haven's Place."

Callan does the honors and pulls the cords to reveal the sign. It's huge and beautiful. A cozy feeling comes over me as I stare at it with my mouth hanging open. Overwhelmed, all I can get out is "King…"

Everyone around us congratulates us, and King whisks me away inside.

He kisses my ear and whispers to me, "Do you love it?"

I'm at a loss for words. "I love it… but King, it's too much."

He grabs me by the shoulders. "It's yours, Haven. I've already signed the paperwork. The community center is yours. You can hire someone to work it for you or whatever you want to do."

"But—" I start, and he stops me.

"Listen, the light and happiness you've brought to my life… I'll never take that for granted. This place… I've seen the way you love it, and I want you to have it. You'll do amazing things with it."

I grab on to the front of his shirt. "But I want us to do it together. This is something we could do together."

"I will be by your side every step of the way. I will be as much—or as little—involved as you want me to be. I know how important this is to you, and I want you to have something that is yours."

I go on my tiptoes and loop my arms around King's neck. My body is flush against his, but his hands go to my ass, and he holds me to him. My fingers thread through the hair at the nape of his neck. "I told you last night that the only thing I need is you."

He leans his forehead against mine. "You have me. You will always have me."

"I love you, husband."

He leans down and whispers, "I love you, my wife." And then he kisses me until I have no doubts exactly how he feels about me.

EPILOGUE
KING

Two Months Later

I PULL at my suit jacket and stare out at the crowd. It seems like everyone is here. Well, everyone except for my brother, Ledger. He's somewhere in a foreign country, and he couldn't make it back in time. But Holden, Dom, Gabe, and Chrissy are all here, and they know what my plans are for tonight. It's supposed to be a party, celebrating Haven and my marriage, but I'm hoping it's more. My wife is laughing with her friends, and I try to hide my nervousness as I walk over to her. As I get to her, I put my arms around her, and she leans into me. "Hey, wife."

She smiles up at me. "Hey, husband."

I look at her friend, Cassie. "Thank you for putting this all together. It's perfect."

Cassie claps her hands together, and I know she's excited because she knows what's about to happen. Hopefully, Haven will just think it's because of the party she's so happy.

The community center is full. No matter how hard I tried, Haven was determined to have the party here. I'm hoping she won't regret it later. As I look around, I'm amazed at the transformation of the place.

I hold my hand out to her. "Want to come up front with me? I need to make a speech."

She scrunches up her nose. It's always amazing to me how she's a model, but she doesn't like to have attention on herself. But she puts her hand in mine. "I'll go anywhere with you, Mr. Beckett."

As we make our way to the front, people stop us to congratulate us, and I can't help thinking about how different my life is now with Haven in it. I was just getting by before she came along. Yeah, I had money, more money than I'll ever need, but nothing compares to having Haven's love. She has made my whole life better.

When we finally make it to the front, Callan is standing there with a microphone, and he pins it to my shirt. I turn to the crowd and start to talk. "Hey, everybody. Can I get your attention?"

People stop talking, and with Haven's hand in mine, I thank everyone for coming. "Haven and I wanted to thank each and every one of you for joining us today. You know, she became my wife a few months ago in a rushed ceremony. I was so afraid she'd change her mind that I sort of sprang it on her. I don't regret anything about that day, in my mind it was perfect."

I turn and look at my wife and continue talking. "I know you said that you didn't need the big wedding, but I'm hoping you'll humor me. We don't have any pictures from our wedding, since none of our family or friends were there to witness it."

"I was there," Chrissy hollers out.

I chuckle. "Well, my sister was there, of course, but I want us to do it again and do it right this time." I get down on one knee. "Haven, you are everything to me, and I love our life together. I know that you are already my wife, but I'm hoping that you'll marry me in front of our family and friends. Will you marry me… again?"

Haven looks so happy, and it's only then that I knew I made the right decision. I don't know why this is so important to me. Maybe I still worry that I cheated her with our rushed wedding in our living room.

She goes to her knees in front of me and wraps her arms around my neck. "You know I will, King. I love you."

I hold on to her as the room erupts in cheers.

I help her up, and Holden comes forward. I put my hand on my brother's shoulder. "I hope you're okay with it. Holden's going to walk you down the aisle to me."

Her eyes are shiny with wetness as she looks at Holden. "Thank you. I would love that."

In most people's eyes, my brother is considered a player, but he is completely enamored by my wife and is taking his job very seriously. He looks at Haven proudly. "No, sweetie, it will be my honor to do it." There's been a change in my brother recently. A few weeks ago, he told me he was jealous of what Haven and I have, and he wants to settle down. It's hard for me to picture, but I'm ready for him to prove me wrong.

I kiss Haven. "I'll be right here waiting for you."

She walks away with Holden, and I take my

place next to the pastor, who is now standing in the front. My other brothers stand next to me, and after I hug each of them, I wait for my wife to come.

The music comes on, and my sister Chrissy walks out first. Next, Haven's friend Cassie walks down the aisle. When they're both at the front, I take a deep breath as the wedding march comes over the speakers. Everyone stands up, but I only have eyes for Haven. Someone has attached a veil to her head, and she and Holden make their way down the aisle. I meet them at the end, and Holden kisses her cheek and grasps my shoulder. Then I take my wife in my arms.

The pastor performs the ceremony, and I can't take my eyes off my beautiful wife. When it's time to put the ring on her finger, she gasps when she sees the four-carat ring I picked out for her. She moves her first wedding band to her other hand, and I put the new one on her finger. As soon as the pastor pronounces us husband and wife, I take her in my arms and kiss her until we're both breathless.

After the ceremony, we stand at the back of the room as everyone comes and congratulates us. There's food, dancing, laughter, and fellowship. The night is perfect.

When Haven and I are dancing, I hold her close. "Were you surprised?"

"Yes, I had no idea, and I loved it. I can't believe you planned all this."

"Chrissy and Cassie were a big help."

"I still can't believe it. Thank you for thinking of it. I love that we're getting to celebrate with all our family and friends."

Haven

I am still shocked that he was able to pull this off. I have my own surprise that I planned to tell him later, but now seems a good as time as any.

"I have something for you too."

"You didn't have to get me anything. Having you as my wife is more than enough."

I laugh and loop my arms around his neck. My body is flush with his, and his manhood is digging into my belly, but I don't care if the room is full of people, I'm going to enjoy this. "I think you're going to want this, King."

He locks his hands at my back. "Of course I'll want anything you give me."

I lean up to tell him. My lips graze his ear, and he trembles. I laugh. "Hold still. You don't want to miss this." I lean into his arms. "You're going to be a dad."

He freezes and pulls back to look in my face. "What did you just say?"

I am smiling ear to ear. "You're going to be a dad. I'm pregnant, King."

His hands go to my waist. "We're going to have a baby?"

He's stunned, and I nod my head. "Yes."

He picks me up in his arms and swings me around in circles. He stops suddenly, puts me on my feet, and then places a hand to my belly. "Oh my God, I'm sorry. Are you okay? Is the baby okay?"

"We're fine. It's okay."

He starts to lead me off the dance floor. "Should you sit down?"

I smack his chest playfully. "Oh no, Mr. Beckett. You are not going to get fussy. I'm good. I'm feeling good. I may have to take time off from modeling for a while, but—"

He searches my eyes worriedly. "Are you okay with that?"

I bite my lip and nod. "Yeah. I told you that I was going to retire soon. It just may be sooner than later. I'm good with it, King. I'm about to have our baby."

He clenches his eyes closed, overcome with emotion. "Thank you, Haven. Thank you for showing me what true love is. Thank you for loving me and not giving up on me. I love you so much."

"I love you, too."

EXTENDED EPILOGUE
THE HONEYMOON

Haven

And the surprises just keep coming.

King not only arranged a wedding but also surprised me with a honeymoon.

We're now in Hawaii, and I'm lounging on a chair with the crystal clear blue ocean in front of me.

I lean back in my chair, letting the sun beat down on me as I hold my book in my hands. I feel like I've been on a high since the surprise wedding. There are people all around us, but anytime I'm with King, he treats me like I'm the only woman in the room.

I lift up, shade my eyes to look for my husband,

and see him walking back to me. He has his hands full, and his gaze is set on me, but it's almost comical the way every woman he passes stares at him and watches him walk by.

I'm not laughing, though, because I'm territorial when it comes to my husband.

He's smiling at me the whole way, and when he sits down on the chair next to mine, he holds out my drink. "Bahama Mama, no alcohol."

"Thank you." I take a big drink and try to avert my eyes from his bare chest. I'm not sure if it's the pregnancy hormones or what it is, but lately I can't get enough of King.

"What's wrong?"

I'm not sure if I'm itching to pick a fight or what, but I point in the direction he just came from. "Did you see all those women looking at you?"

He reaches over and puts his hand on my knee. "No, because I had my eyes on one woman."

I huff out a breath. I point out the group of women that all have their heads turned to watch my husband. "Look, even now, they're still looking for you, trying to see where you went."

I have no reason to be jealous. King is all about me and making me feel loved, so I'm not sure why I'm acting the way I am.

His hand trails a little higher up my knee. "I think you should forget about them. You know what might help?"

I sigh in frustration. "What?"

He moves over to my chair, facing me, and sits next to my hip. He's hovering over me, just watching me.

"What are you looking at?"

The gold flecks in his eyes darken. "You know what I'm looking at."

My heart is fluttering uncontrollably. It's crazy the way my body reacts to him, and I keep waiting for the desire to fade, but it's nowhere near lessening. If anything, I want him more and more.

"Tell me, Haven. What am I looking at?"

"My pretty mouth."

He traces his finger around my lips. "Yep, I'm thinking about the way that pretty mouth was wrapped around my dick this morning. You took me so good. I'm still half hard from it."

My pulse picks up. This isn't fair. What I did to him was in the privacy of our room. He's talking all this dirty talk, and he can't do nothing about it out here. "You're not being fair, King."

His hand goes higher and traces along the edge of my bathing suit. With each pass of his thumb across my sensitive skin, my pussy tightens. "You need me to take care of you, peaches?"

My legs widen because he's right. That's exactly what I need, but as soon as his finger traces over my bathing suit at the seam of my pussy, I snap my legs closed. "Argh, I should have let you rent that cabana, King."

He leans down and gestures behind us. "You mean that cabana?"

I gasp and look behind me, finding the cabana still empty. "You didn't?"

He stands up, holding his hand out to me. "I did."

We walk over to the cabana, and it feels like all eyes are on us. A part of me is hoping that the gaggle of women see him walking with me into the cabana. He points at the couch. "Lie down."

I do as I'm told as King pulls the curtains closed. He leaves about a foot of the curtains open, and I lean up on my arms. "Are you going to close them?"

He shakes his head side to side.

"But—"

He reaches for the bottoms of my bikini. "You think I'll let someone see you?"

There's one thing I know about King: He's

protective. He's not going to let anyone see me like this. He drops my bottoms on the other couch. "You trust me?"

"You know I do."

He leans over to kiss me and then trails kisses down my body. Every inch of skin he passes feels electric. When he puts his hands on my inner thighs and pushes them apart, I take in a deep breath.

He's licking his lips as he looks at me. "You have a pretty pussy, peaches."

He parts my slit, sliding his finger through my swollen cunt.

My hips thrust, needing his touch, and he doesn't let me down. His finger pumps in and out of me, and I whimper.

He slows his hand. "You going to be a good girl for me? You have to be quiet. Can you do that?"

I moan my response, and there's no telling what it is I said, but he doesn't seem to mind. He strokes me, bringing out another moan that's louder this time. "I'm going to taste you now." He fits his mouth over my pussy and licks me until I orgasm right here on the public beach. His masterful tongue is my undoing.

When I'm able to catch my breath, he pulls me

to his lap. His cock is hard against my hip, and I wrap my hand around him. "I need you inside me."

He has me up so fast he has to help me get steady on my feet. He holds out my bikini bottoms, and I step into them, then he pulls them up my legs. As soon as they're on, he's patting my sensitive pussy. "We're going to the room."

He holds onto my hand and has us practically running through the sand. I'm huffing and puffing when he finally slows down. "Shit, I'm sorry, Haven. You okay?" He cups his hand to my belly. "Is the baby okay?"

I nod, burrowing into his side. "The baby is fine… it's me you have to worry about."

He stops walking and looks frantic. "What is it? Are you hurting? Shit, I shouldn't have—"

I loop my arms around his neck and my nipples are hard. I know my bathing suit top is doing nothing to hide my arousal. "The only thing I need is you, my King, deep inside me. That's all I meant… I'm tired of waiting."

Without another word, he walks us to the elevator. As soon as the door shuts us inside, he's on me. His hands are everywhere, and I wrap my leg around his thigh, needing him closer.

The elevator dings, and we pull apart. We step

off the elevator, and he fumbles the key card to get us inside. Once in, he's pulling my clothes off until I'm naked. He follows suit, and his cock is hard, standing straight up.

I waste no time climbing on the bed, and before I can turn around, King grabs my hips and pulls me to the edge. He lines himself up and pummels into me with one possessive stroke. A guttural groan leaves me, and he stops.

"You okay?"

I'm catching my breath as I look at him over my shoulder. "I need you to fuck me, deep and hard, King. Make me yours."

"You are mine." He grunts as he drives into me. Over and over he takes me, and he doesn't stop until both of us are consumed by orgasms that wrack our entire bodies.

He groans, lying on me and covering my back. His voice is commanding in my ear. "Fuck, I love you."

I try to catch my breath. I went from never having anyone touch me or love me to a man that shows me love in every way. "I love you too."

Whiskey Run: Heroes

Ransom - He's on a mission he can't lose.

Redeem - He's in love with his sister's best friend.

Submit - She's his fake wife but he wants to make it real.

Forbid - They have a secret romance but he's about to stake his claim.

Whiskey Run: Sugar

One Night Love - Her one night stand wants more.

Rebound Love - She's falling for the rebound guy.

Second Chance Love - He is not a man to ignore... especially when he asks for a second chance.

Bad Boy Love - He's a bad boy that wants her good.

Whiskey Run: Guardians MC

Protective Biker - She needs his protection and he'll give it to her. But he's going to need her heart in exchange.

Broken Biker - There's only one woman for him…

Relentless Biker - He won't stop until he has her back.

Whiskey Men

Reluctant Husband - If you love reading about curvy women getting the hot guy, opposites attract, jealousy trope, marriage of convenience, and small-town romance, then you'll love Lucas and Isabella's story.

Something Real - If you love reading billionaire, single

father, age gap, boss/employee, and small-town romance, then you'll love Ford and Lilian's story.

Coming Home - If you love reading billionaire, ex-military, age gap, forced proximity, and small-town romance, then you'll love Hudson and Elle's story.

Forever Mine - If you love reading billionaire, age gap, second chance, and small-town romance, then you'll love Beau and Natalie's story.

Always Yours - If you love reading billionaire, friends to lovers, pregnancy, and small town romance, then you'll love Austin and Ally's story.

Whiskey Men: Wounded Heroes

Sweet Addiction - Curvy Single Mom and the Wounded Hero. Together in a brother's best friend romance.

Dark Obsession - Curvy Divorcee and the Wounded Hero. Together in an against all odds romance.

Unbreakable Bond - Curvy woman and the Wounded Hero. Together in an age gap, best friend's daughter romance.

Scarred Promises - A one night stand with the wounded hero.

JOIN ME!

JOIN MY NEWSLETTER

www.AuthorHopeFord.com/Subscribe

ABOUT THE AUTHOR

Hope Ford is a USA Today Bestselling author of Steamy, Sweet, Satisfying Romance.

She loves writing about small towns, swoony men, and curvy women that get their happily-ever-after.

To find me on Pinterest, Instagram, Facebook, Goodreads, and more:

www.AuthorHopeFord.com/follow-me

Want **FREE BOOKS?**
Go to www.authorhopeford.com/freebies